VAN HELSING™

THE JUNIOR NOVEL

VAN HELSING™

THE JUNIOR NOVEL

BY CARLA JABLONSKI

ADAPTED FROM A MOTION PICTURE

SCREENPLAY WRITTEN BY

STEPHEN SOMMERS

HarperFestival®

A Division of HarperCollins*Publishers*

P R O L O G U E

T hunder roared as lightning shattered the night sky. The calamitous storm nearly drowned out the shouts of the crazed mob storming Castle Frankenstein. Dr. Victor Frankenstein took no notice as he concentrated on his grand experiment, his greatest triumph as a scientist. He gazed down at the enormous man strapped into an iron pod in front of him. The man wore a metal cap with electrical wires running from it up to the rafters and out to conductors on the roof.

All of Dr. Frankenstein's research and sacrifices had led to this moment. He was so close. Just a few more seconds for the lightning to do its work, and victory would be his.

Another crash of lightning; another pounding on

the heavy wooden doors far below. More shouts calling for his head. The scientist ignored it all, riveted by the man's tiny fluttering movements. Then—it happened. The man's eyes flew open. They locked onto Dr. Frankenstein's, and the scientist trembled. He felt as if the creature had peered into his very soul.

"He's alive!" Dr. Frankenstein cried, adding his voice to the mad chorus of sounds in the frantic night. He threw back his head and held out his arms wide, chortling in glee. "He's *aliiive*!"

"Success!" a voice rang out in the darkness.

Dr. Frankenstein spun around, startled and frightened. He had thought he was alone. Who could have gotten into his laboratory at the very top of his turreted castle?

A tall figure stepped forward out of the shadows.

"Ah, Count Dracula, it's you." Dr. Frankenstein pulled a handkerchief from his pocket and mopped his sweaty forehead. "You caught me by surprise."

"I was beginning to lose faith, Doctor," the count said. "But I see you have achieved your marvelous dream."

A loud crash outside kept Dr. Frankenstein from replying. He hurried to the window and peered down. The townspeople below were pounding a sturdy tree

trunk into his front door. He knew that it would not hold much longer. He was stunned to see that there were hundreds of villagers, their fury clearly visible in the light from their flaming torches.

A scrawny man with ragged white hair leapt up onto a boulder. "You know what he is doing up there?" he shouted in a grating, high-pitched voice. He waved his battered top hat toward the turret. "How he is experimenting with the bodies of your dearly departed! We must stop him!"

"A pity your moment of triumph is being spoiled over a little charge of grave robbery," Dracula said to Dr. Frankenstein.

"One, two, three. Now!" the crowd shouted, ramming the tree into the heavy door once more. The man with the top hat cackled demonically. He practically danced on top of the boulder, firing up the crowd.

Fear rushed through Dr. Frankenstein as he gazed at the enraged throng below him. "Yes. Yes. I must escape this place."

"Again!" the townspeople shouted.

Dr. Frankenstein dashed across the lab and threw open a large trunk beside his desk. "What do I take? What do I leave behind?" he muttered. He stood and looked around the crowded laboratory, at a loss for how to proceed.

"Where are you going to run to?" Dracula asked, moving closer.

Instinctively, Dr. Frankenstein backed up, banging into the trunk. The count had always made him nervous, and he was already on edge. Dracula, handsome, elegant, and imposing, radiated something that Dr. Frankenstein could not ignore. He reeked of evil.

"Your peculiar experiments have made you unwelcome in the civilized world, Victor," Dracula continued, his voice smooth and calm.

Dr. Frankenstein looked at the iron pod again. The man was watching his every movement. Dr. Frankenstein's heart clutched; there seemed to be such pleading in those recently dead eyes.

"I'll take him away. Far away, where no one will ever find him," Dr. Frankenstein said defiantly.

He grabbed several books and turned to place them in the trunk, but Dracula was suddenly right beside him. The count stepped on the lid of the trunk, slamming it shut.

"No, Victor," Dracula countered. "The time has come for me to take command of him."

"What are you saying?" Dr. Frankenstein asked.

"Why do you think I brought you here? Gave you this castle? Equipped your lab?"

"Y—y—you said you believed in my w—work," Dr. Frankenstein stammered.

Dracula smiled. "And I do. But now that you have completed your experiment, it is time for your work to serve my purpose."

"What purpose?"

In one fluid movement, Dracula leapt up and perched in the rafters. Dr. Frankenstein's mouth dropped open in astonishment and he started backing away.

"No," Dr. Frankenstein gasped. "I would kill myself before helping you in any task."

"Feel free," Dracula said. "I don't actually need you anymore. I just need him." He gestured to the man in the iron pod. He dropped back down to the floor, inches from Dr. Frankenstein.

Dr. Frankenstein set his jaw and narrowed his eyes. "Before I would allow him to be used for such evil, I would destroy him."

"I cannot allow that to happen," Dracula said. "My brides would be most upset."

Dr. Frankenstein knew he was trapped. He could never fight Dracula on his own. "Igor!" he cried. "Igor, help me!" He frantically scanned the lab for his servant. He spotted the thuggish, misshapen hunchback up in the rafters.

Igor pushed his long, straggly hair over his shoulder. He grinned, revealing his crooked, rotting teeth, contorting his grotesque features even more. "I'm sorry, Doctor. You've been so kind to me. But if that mob catches me, they'll hang me all over again."

His panic rising, Dr. Frankenstein reached back and grabbed a saber crossed over the Frankenstein coat of arms that hung on the wall above the mantel. He brandished the sword at Dracula. "Stay back," he ordered.

The count walked straight toward Dr. Frankenstein. The scientist could only gape in astonishment as he watched Dracula continue his approach, impaling himself up to the hilt on the saber. "You can't kill me, Victor." Dracula sneered. "I'm already dead."

Dr. Frankenstein's stomach lurched as much from fear as from the horrible stench of death now emanating from the count. His knees buckled as he watched the count's face grow pale and his teeth change into razor-sharp fangs.

"Say good-bye to your creator," Dracula hissed to the man strapped to the table. Then he sank his teeth into Dr. Frankenstein's neck.

"Nooo!"

The anguished cry behind him startled Dracula,

and he dropped Dr. Frankenstein to the floor. The scientist's creation burst from the straps holding him down. "No!" he bellowed again. He hurled a heavy, metal coil at Dracula, smashing the count in the head. Dracula stumbled backward into the fireplace, sending sparks and ashes flying everywhere.

The huge man gathered Dr. Frankenstein's dead body in his arms. "Father!" he wailed.

Instinct took over. Somehow the creature knew he had to protect himself and his creator. He lifted the limp body and charged out of the laboratory and out of the castle.

Igor raced to a balcony and watched the creature's progress. Down below, the villagers had broken through the doorway of the castle and were swarming inside. Others still hurled rocks up at the windows. Igor cupped his hands around his twisted mouth and shouted above their cries. "Frankenstein has created a monster!"

No one seemed to hear him. No one but the thin man in the top hat perched on top of a large boulder.

The man in the top hat looked up at Igor, then in the direction Igor was pointing. An enormous man— no, a *monster*—was stumbling across the dark moors.

"Look!" he screamed, waving his top hat to get attention. "Look! It's heading for the windmill!"

The villagers stopped their invasion of the castle and began to chase after the hulking figure in the night.

The creature could hear the thudding footsteps, the shouts, the crackling fire of the torches behind him and he ran as fast as he could. The damp mud of the moors slowed him down, but he fought against the clinging dirt and made it to the abandoned windmill. Still the mob charged after him.

He burst through the windmill's shattered door and raced up the rickety wooden staircase. He lumbered to the top of the windmill, still clutching the dead body of Dr. Frankenstein.

A crash of lightning illuminated him for a moment—every bolt, every stitch, every scar clearly visible to the crazed mob below. A small electrical storm was going off inside the back of his head as he tried to understand what was happening—and tried to fight the terror raging through him.

"Why?" Frankenstein's monster moaned. "Why?"

"Get him!" someone shouted.

The creature's terror grew as the villagers hurled torches at the wooden windmill. A noose of flame leapt up the structure's walls. The monster roared in fear.

A shattering sound from across the moors ripped

his attention from the growing fire. The skylight in Frankenstein's castle had exploded. Dark shadows high up in the thunder-raked sky flew through the roiling purple clouds straight toward the windmill.

Gasps rippled through the mob. "Vampires!" someone cried. "Run for your lives!"

The huge crowd fled in horror across the moors. The flames surged up the windmill, surrounding the creature. He gazed down at Dr. Frankenstein's lifeless body and hugged him tightly to his enormous chest.

"Father," the creature whispered. Then, with tears streaming down his scarred cheeks, he lifted a fist toward the oncoming vampires and let out an anguished bellow.

BOOM! The windmill imploded, the timber and gears and ironwork plummeting down into itself, taking the creature and Dr. Frankenstein down too. Flaming debris flew everywhere.

Dracula and his brides swooped down to the ground. Transforming quickly from their gigantic bat forms, the brides burst into tears, wailing with inhuman shrieks. Dracula staggered a few steps toward the flaming wreckage and could only stare in disbelief.

One year later . . .
Prince Velkan, son of Boris Valerious, the dead

king of the gypsies, tensed at a crackling in the bushes just beyond the clearing. His head whipped in the direction of the sound. His movement forced his wrists to strain against the straps that bound him to the post. Another branch creaked. Leaves rustled. Velkan's every sense was heightened as he waited for the inevitable attack.

"Show yourself," he murmured.

He caught his breath as the massive ten-foot-tall beast appeared, creeping along a thick low branch, its yellow eyes boring into Velkan's, its sharp fangs and claws glistening as it prepared to attack. The dreaded werewolf.

The creature hunkered down, gathering its energy, preparing to lunge.

Velkan's brown eyes narrowed. "Come on. Dracula unleashed you for a reason," he muttered.

The werewolf leapt!

At the last possible moment Velkan ripped his hands from their bindings, and vaulted himself onto the top of the post.

Wham! The werewolf slammed into it, exactly where Velkan had stood only moments ago, attempting to lure the beast to attack. The animal dug its claws into the post and glared up at Velkan, fury flashing in its eyes.

Velkan grabbed thick vines hanging above the post. He wrapped them around his wrists. "Now!" he cried.

The men hidden in the bushes pulled a lever. The vines around Velkan's wrists went taut, and they jerked him up above the pole. After a moment, he came to an abrupt stop. "What's wrong?" he shouted.

"It's stuck!" one of the men in the bushes shouted. "The lever is stuck!"

Velkan glanced down and saw the werewolf gripping the pole not far below him. The creature was preparing to lunge again.

A movement in the bushes near the lever caught Velkan's eye. A gorgeous young woman in a close-fitting red jacket and black pants stepped into the clearing, ready to draw her sword.

A man behind her gripped her arm, trying to drag her back. "No!" the man cried. "The werewolf will kill you!"

The woman yanked her arm out of the man's grasp. "That's my brother out there!"

The werewolf growled as its attention went from Velkan to the woman.

"Anna! Go back!" Velkan shouted at his sister, Anna Valerious.

Without a word in reply Anna brandished her

sword and charged the werewolf. The beast snarled viciously and leapt down from the pole. It landed—and instantly plummeted through a camouflaged mesh covering the ground. At the same moment, a man in the bushes swung an axe. It crashed down onto the ropes attached to the lever. A huge iron cage ripped out of the ground around the pole, and was pulled high into the air.

The werewolf was trapped inside.

Still clinging to the vine, Velkan drew his silver revolver. He aimed it toward the rising cage, trying to keep steady on the swinging vine. As the cage pulled up next to Velkan, the werewolf slammed against the cage's bars. The force of its movement knocked the cage right into Velkan. Velkan's gun went flying.

"Oh, no!" Velkan cried. "My gun!"

The cage slammed to a stop way up in the trees. It swung wildly back and forth as the werewolf howled and flung itself against the bars. The ropes holding it aloft creaked and snapped.

"Find my gun!" Velkan ordered.

Down below, Anna desperately looked around. Several men charged out of the bushes, readied their rifles and took aim at the cage.

"No!" Anna shoved a man aside, causing his shot to go wild. "We must find Velkan's gun! We can only

use the silver bullets!"

Anna heard another rope snap. She peered up to the treetops and gasped. The cage was hanging from a single rope! Her wide dark eyes scanned the clearing. "There it is!" she cried.

She raced toward the sparkling silver gun lying on the other side of the clearing. She'd made it halfway across the grass when—*wham*—the huge cage slammed onto the ground in front of her, blocking her from the gun. The cage buckled and splintered, and the werewolf burst out of it.

Anna whirled around and ran, her long brown hair streaming out behind her. She headed for the forest—but she knew the werewolf was right behind her.

Anna pumped her legs harder and she leapt over tree roots and ducked under branches. She burst out of the other side of the forest and came to a sudden, gasping stop. One more step and she would have flown right over the edge of the cliff.

She took in a few breaths, her heart pounding hard. *I have to find cover*, she told herself. She dashed toward a path leading back into another part of the woods.

A loud crash made her freeze. She slowly turned around and her mouth dropped open. Trees and

bushes flew into the air as the enormous werewolf cleared a path toward her.

Anna backed up and gripped her sword. The werewolf charged out of the bushes heading straight for her. As Anna clutched her sword tighter, her brother Velkan barreled down the path toward her and shoved her to the ground.

Anna heard Velkan fire his silver gun over and over as the creature howled in pain. But when she scrambled back to her feet, the werewolf and her brother had both vanished from sight!

All that was left was the silver gun lying on the ground, still smoking.

"Oh, Velkan," Anna moaned, staring over the cliff where he must have fallen along with the werewolf. Slowly, painfully, she stood up. She brushed her long dark hair out of her eyes—then froze at a crackling sound coming from the bushes. Anna crept toward the noise. She held Velkan's silver gun out in front of her and parted the branches with it.

"Werewolf!" she snarled. She cocked the gun and aimed it at the wounded creature.

But before she could get off a shot, the creature transformed into a pitiful, dying old man.

"Thank you," the man gasped. "I can die free of Dracula's awful grip."

Anna stared down at the man, who gazed up at her with pale, milky eyes. He gripped her ankle with the last strength he had. "You must stop him," the old man pleaded. "He has a terrible secret. He has—" The man coughed. "He has . . . he has . . ." At last his fingers released Anna's ankle and his head dropped back. He was dead.

Anna knelt down beside the old man. "Don't worry," she promised. "I will find Dracula—and destroy him once and for all!"

ONE

Van Helsing strode along the rainy cobblestone street, admiring the progress being made on the Eiffel Tower. *They should have that thing finished in a few months*, he thought.

A "wanted" poster recently plastered to a brick wall caught his attention. A familiar pair of eyes stared out at him. Van Helsing stepped up to the wall for a closer look. The man depicted was wanted for murder.

"A rather handsome fellow," Van Helsing noted, taking in the man's mask, long dark hair, broad-shouldered cloak, and wide-brimmed black hat.

He ran a finger along the brim of his own, identical, black hat. He flung one side of his cloak over his shoulder, then ripped the poster from the wall, crumpled it, and tossed it into the street.

"I suppose I'll need to leave Paris now," he murmured, strolling over one of the bridges that crossed the Seine. "I've become a bit too visible here."

*   *   *

A few days later, Van Helsing sat in a small confessional in a chapel in Vatican City, Rome. He jiggled his foot and gritted his teeth as he waited for the lecture he had coming to him. He didn't have to wait long.

The little door in the wooden panel slid open with a bang. Van Helsing couldn't see much of Cardinal Jinette, but he could easily picture the fury on the tough old man's grizzled face.

"You crashed through a window at Notre Dame!" Cardinal Jinette fumed.

"Not to split hairs," Van Helsing replied mildly, "but it was Dr. Jekyll—or was it Mr. Hyde?—who actually did the crashing. I just followed after him."

Cardinal Jinette continued. "Thirteenth century. Over six hundred years old! I wish you a week in hell for that."

"It would be a nice reprieve," Van Helsing muttered.

The cardinal made a few *tsk*ing sounds as he shook his head. "Don't get me wrong. Your results are undeniable, but you draw far too much attention to yourself."

Van Helsing shrugged. "I do what I have to do."

"*Wanted* posters!" Cardinal Jinette exclaimed. "You were to keep a low profile, and what happens? Your methods result in *wanted* posters! Your face, your name,

spread all over the city. No—several cities!"

Van Helsing could feel himself getting angry. "Do you think I like being the most wanted man in Europe?" he demanded. "Why don't you and the Order do something about it?"

Cardinal Jinette leaned toward the window and lowered his voice. "You know why," he snapped. "Because the Order does not exist."

"Then neither do I," Van Helsing snapped back. He stood and reached for the doorknob.

Then he heard a click. He tested the door to the confessional and shook his head. The cardinal had triggered a bolt to lock the door from the outside. Apparently, the conversation was not over.

"When we found you crawling up the steps of this very church, half dead, it was clear to us that you had been sent to do this work," Cardinal Jinette said.

"Why don't you just do it yourself?" Van Helsing grumbled.

The cardinal shot Van Helsing a sharp look. "Do not disrespect me or the Order. You have already lost your memory as penance for your past sins." His face moved away from the small window, and a moment later the confessional wall slid away, revealing a staircase.

Cardinal Jinette addressed Van Helsing from the top of the stairs. "If you wish to recover that memory,

I suggest you continue to heed your calling. With us."

Deep down, Van Helsing knew that the cardinal did truly appreciate the risks he took for the cause. So he dropped the argument and followed Cardinal Jinette down the dark stone staircase.

They soon reached an enormous underground cavern housing the secret armory of the Order. Representatives from all of the worlds' religions bustled about. They were hard at work, creating the tools and weapons of their shared mission: to rid the world of evil.

Cardinal Jinette and Van Helsing made their way past the huge furnaces where rabbis worked the bellows while Hindu priests stoked the flames. Muslim clerics pounded red-hot scimitars on iron anvils. Catholic priests toiled beside Kabbalistic mystics pouring lead, silver, gold, and copper into molds. The place rang with the sounds of hammers and anvils, hissing steam and shouts.

Cardinal Jinette stopped to scan the scene approvingly. "Governments and empires rise and fall," he said. "But we have kept mankind safe since time immemorial. We are the last defense against the kind of evil that the rest of mankind, thankfully, has no idea even exists."

Van Helsing nodded. He knew the importance of the work, but he wondered if the Order understood

what the missions cost him.

"To you, these monsters are evil beings to be vanquished," he said to Cardinal Jinette, trying to explain. "But I'm the one left standing there when they die. I'm the one who witnesses their return to the men they had once been. You see, at the moment of death, they all do. They become human again, and I've killed them."

Cardinal Jinette put his hand on Van Helsing's shoulder. "I know this weighs heavily on you," he said sympathetically. "But it is only in death that they can be freed from the monsters that imprison them. And it is only in the demise of such creatures that mankind can be safe."

Van Helsing sighed. The cardinal was right; this was his calling. Unfortunately the pain it caused him could not be lightened by kind words from the cardinal.

"So what's my mission now?" Van Helsing asked. He hoped that focusing on the next task, getting back into action quickly would help him shake his melancholy mood.

The cardinal stopped in front of a wall and snapped his fingers. A rabbi scurried into place behind a slide projector, and the lights dimmed. A map appeared projected on the wall, indicating the route between Rome and a small principality in Eastern Europe.

"We need you to go to the east," the cardinal explained. "To the far side of Romania. It is an accursed land, terrorized by all sorts of nightmarish creatures. Lorded over by this man."

Another picture appeared on the wall. This was a portrait of a handsome man with long dark hair pulled back in a sleek ponytail. "Count Dracula," Cardinal Jinette intoned.

"Dracula," Van Helsing repeated. The name sent a shiver of recognition through him.

Dracula's image vanished, and a new one took its place. This was of a painting depicting a knight in armor holding up a sword. The name VALERIOUS THE ELDER was emblazoned on the frame of the painting. Van Helsing waited for the cardinal to make some connection between this fifteenth-century nobleman and the count in the previous slide.

Cardinal Jinette gazed up at the portrait. "Four hundred and fifty years ago," he explained, "a Transylvanian knight named Valerious the Elder took holy vows that his family would never rest, nor would they ever enter heaven, until they had vanquished Dracula. In all these generations, they have not succeeded. They are running out of family."

The cardinal snapped his fingers, and other pictures appeared. These looked like family photos. Van

Helsing studied a burly man, a young prince, and a girl on horseback.

Cardinal Jinette tapped the image of the older man. "Boris Valerious, king of the gypsies, went missing about a year ago." He pointed to the younger man. "His son, Velkan, died last week."

"And the girl?" Van Helsing asked.

"Princess Anna. The last of the Valeriouses. The last hope of her family."

He snapped his fingers once more, and the armory filled with light. "For more than four centuries this family has given their lives to this cause. Our cause. We cannot let them stay stranded in purgatory."

Van Helsing nodded, knowing where this was heading. "And that's where I come in."

"Yes." Cardinal Jinette waved an old Muslim cleric forward. The elderly gentleman handed something to the cardinal, who then held it up for Van Helsing to see. It was a torn piece of painted cloth, encased in glass.

"What's this?" Van Helsing asked, taking it from the cardinal to examine it more closely.

"The old knight left this here four hundred years ago," the Cardinal explained. "We don't know its purpose, but he would not have left it without a good reason."

Van Helsing pointed to an inscription on the cloth. "What does this say? My Latin is rusty."

"It translates as 'In the name of God, open this door.'"

Van Helsing peered at the cloth, then his eyes widened. There, in the corner of the ancient, frayed fabric was an insignia in the shape of a dragon, the same insignia decorating the heavy gold ring Van Helsing wore on his right hand.

Cardinal Jinette touched Van Helsing's shoulder. "I think you might find the answers you seek in Transylvania," he said softly.

TWO

Van Helsing stood in the center of the armory, watching the activity around him.

"There you are!" A small, earnest friar scurried to greet Van Helsing. "I've got everything you need."

"In a minute, Carl." Van Helsing pushed past the stocky young man, intrigued by the glowing swords being pulled out of the flaming forge.

"Any idiot can make a sword," Carl scoffed, rolling his eyes.

A huge Buddhist monk with a shaved head stepped out from behind the forge, his thick body covered with sweat. He gripped the red-hot metal in his iron tongs and glared at Carl.

Carl smiled broadly. "Sorry, father, nothing personal."

Carl quickly tugged on Van Helsing's cloak and they both hurried away. They stopped at a row of

shelves filled with canisters, jars, and boxes.

"Let's see." Carl rummaged through the collection, his blond head bobbing up and down as he searched various shelves. "Some of this, yes, and that . . . Uh-huh. That couldn't hurt. Mm-mmm. Yes. This should do it."

He turned to Van Helsing. "Okay, you've got your holy water, silver crucifix, rings of garlic, and, of course, the ever-popular wooden stake." He dumped all the items into Van Helsing's arms.

"Why can't I have one of those?" Van Helsing gazed back longingly at the Buddhist monk's newly forged swords.

Carl raised an eyebrow. "You've never gone after vampires, have you?"

Van Helsing snorted dismissively. "Vampires, gargoyles, warlocks, they're all the same. Best when cooked well-done!"

"They are *not* all the same," Carl protested. "A vampire is nothing like a warlock. Sheesh! My granny could kill a warlock."

"Carl, you've never been out of the abbey," Van Helsing pointed out. "How do you know about vampires?"

Now it was Carl's turn to scoff. "That's why they make books." He waved at the floor-to-ceiling shelves

lining the opposite wall. They were filled with ancient tomes, recent manuscripts, and everything in between.

"But since you're so smitten with the latest gadgets, here's something new." Carl walked up to a glass oven where sticks of dynamite were dripping sweat into vials. "Glycerin forty-eight," he explained.

Carl stuck his pinky into a vial and then flicked a drop of the dynamite sweat against the wall.

Ka-boom! The droplet burst into a ball of flame. Several of the working clergymen shouted in fear, some dropped to the ground. Then, once they realized what had happened, they all started yelling at Carl.

"Knock it off, Carl."

"We're trying to work here. Quit goofing around."

"You'll get us all killed."

Carl put his hands up in a placating gesture. "Sorry. Sorry," he announced to the room. He stepped in close to Van Helsing. "The air in here is thick with envy," he whispered. Carl put a finger to his lips, indicating that this was their little secret.

"Now," Carl said, back in his normal tone, "let me show you my latest invention." He grabbed a strange-looking crossbow hanging on the wall and handed it to Van Helsing.

Van Helsing had never seen anything like it. The weapon was covered with little iron pumps and copper

tubes. He liked its heft, its balance. And it certainly looked lethal. "Now, this is more like it," Van Helsing said, a grin spreading across his angular face.

"Gas-propelled, capable of catapulting bolts in rapid succession at tremendous velocity," Carl announced. "Just pull the trigger and hold on."

Van Helsing lifted the weapon and peered through the sight, making minor adjustments.

"I've heard the stories coming out of Transylvania," Carl said. "Trust me, you'll need this. A work of certifiable genius."

"If you do say so yourself," Van Helsing teased.

Carl stared at him blankly. "I just said so myself. Didn't you hear me?"

Van Helsing laughed. "Forget it." He lowered the crossbow and spotted a very odd item sitting nearby. "Did you invent this?" he asked.

Carl puffed up with pride. "I've been working on that for twelve years. It's made with compressed magma from Mount Vesuvius and pure alkaline from the Gobi Desert. It's one of a kind."

Curious, Van Helsing picked it up. "What's it for?"

"I have no idea," Carl admitted. "But I'm sure it will come in handy."

Van Helsing raised an eyebrow. "Twelve years of

work and you don't know what it does?"

"I didn't say that," Carl argued. "I said I don't know what it's for. What it does is create a light equal to the intensity of the sun."

"And this will come in handy how?" Van Helsing asked.

Carl shrugged. "I don't know. You could blind your enemies. Charbroil a herd of charging wildebeest. Use your imagination."

Van Helsing gave Carl a long, slow smile. "No, Carl. I'm going to use yours. That's why you're coming with me."

Carl's mouth dropped open, then he started shaking his head vigorously. "Oh, no, I'm not. No way. No how."

"Sorry, Carl. The cardinal has ordered you to keep me alive. Well, for as long as possible."

Van Helsing crossed to the dark corner where he'd stashed the gear he'd been outfitted with so far. He shoved a heavy duffel bag into Carl's arms.

Carl stared at Van Helsing, dumbfounded. "But I'm pure research and development. I don't do the field work."

"I guess you do now," Van Helsing informed him. "Because from now on, where I go, you go."

THREE

"So you can remember everything about your life from the last seven years, but nothing before that?" Carl asked Van Helsing.

"Not now, Carl," Van Helsing said. He scanned the crowd in the town square. Something didn't feel right.

He and Carl had traveled a long way to this small town in Romania. The surrounding craggy mountains and forest cast a gloom over the little village. It was the middle of the afternoon, but the heavy cloud cover and overhanging cliffs and trees made it feel like twilight.

After cosmopolitan Paris and the grand spectacle of Rome, Van Helsing felt as if he'd gone back in time. The village would have seemed quaint if it weren't for the dark and the unmistakable undercurrent of danger.

Van Helsing pulled his hat down low over his eyes and Carl concealed his face under his hooded cloak,

not wanting to attract attention. The locals looked tough—and suspicious.

"There must be *something* you can recall," Carl insisted.

He's not going to get off this topic, Van Helsing thought. "I remember fighting the Romans at Masada," he said.

Carl stopped walking. "That was in seventy-three A.D.!"

Van Helsing looked back over his shoulder. He shrugged. "You asked." He turned back and continued walking.

A gaunt man with ragged white hair and a battered top hat stepped in front of Van Helsing. "Welcome to Transylvania, stranger," the man said in an oily voice. He grinned a nasty grin and rubbed his bony hands together.

When he looked past the man, Van Helsing noticed that the entire crowd had knives, machetes, and pitchforks gripped tightly in their hands.

Carl huddled close behind Van Helsing. "Is it always like this?" he asked nervously.

"Pretty much," Van Helsing replied.

"What are we doing here? Why is it so important to kill this Dracula anyway?"

"Because if we kill him, anything bitten by him or

created by him will also die."

Just then, a beautiful young woman stepped up onto the ledge of the town well, rising above the crowd. Unlike the other women, she wore trousers and tall riding boots. Van Helsing recognized her immediately. She was Anna Valerious, gypsy princess and last of her line.

She tossed her long dark hair over her shoulder. "You!" she called to Van Helsing and Carl. "Let me see your faces."

"Why?" Van Helsing asked.

She put her hands on her hips. "Because we don't trust strangers."

Van Helsing crossed his arms over his chest. "I don't trust anyone."

"Gentlemen, you two will now be disarmed," Anna announced.

Several of the village men moved in closer. Van Helsing stopped them with a glare.

"You can try," he said warningly.

The men shifted their weight, clearly uncertain of what to do.

"You refuse to obey our laws?" Anna demanded.

"The laws of men mean little to me," Van Helsing replied.

"Fine." She gave a sharp nod. "Kill them!"

All the villagers raised their weapons and started closing in on Van Helsing and Carl.

Van Helsing could feel Carl trembling behind him but he didn't budge. "I'm here to help you," Van Helsing told Anna.

"I don't need any help," she informed him.

"Really?" Van Helsing whipped out the crossbow he had slung across his back. Obeying her razor-sharp reflexes, Anna ducked as Van Helsing released the steel bolts at his true targets: three huge, white, bat-like creatures that were flying straight toward Anna! Although their faces were obviously female, as were their body shapes, their enormous, powerful wings, their extremely pointed ears and even *pointier* fangs made it clear that they were far, *far* from human.

Ffft! Fffft! Fffft! Van Helsing shot the bolts one right after the other, but the grotesque white bats were too quick. They split up and soared around the spire of the village church.

"The vampire brides!" The crowd dissolved in chaos as people shrieked, stumbled, and ran in panic. The vampires rocketed around the village square as the crowd became a terrified mob. The churning wind created by the bats' beating wings blew over tables, pulled doors off hinges, and knocked people off their feet.

"Everybody inside!" Anna shouted from atop the well, trying to be heard over the horrified screams.

Van Helsing kept firing his crossbow, but it was hard to take aim in the midst of all the chaos. He didn't want to kill any of the townspeople, but he was determined to stop the vampire bats from doing just that.

One of the evil creatures flew straight at Anna. Just in time, Anna leapt down from her perch. She crashed into Van Helsing, knocking his weapon out of his arms and sending them both sprawling to the ground.

"Normally I don't like women who throw them-selves at me," Van Helsing quipped, trying to catch his breath.

Anna opened her mouth to reply, but her expres-sion changed to one of horror. A vampire bride grabbed her in its talons and yanked her away from Van Helsing and up into the air. Anna dangled from the creature's sharp claws, kicking and cursing in Romanian. "Let go of me, Marishka!" Anna shouted.

Van Helsing scrambled to his feet, jumped up onto the well ledge, and flung himself at Anna. The force knocked her out of the vampire's clutches, and they tumbled to the ground. They each rolled in the dirt, then instantly leapt to their feet.

"I thought you said you didn't need any help," Van Helsing said, grabbing her arm. "Stay here," he ordered.

Anna shot him a dirty look and ripped her arm from his grip. "You stay here. It's me they're trying to kill." She took off running, vanishing behind boxes, barrels, and crates waiting to be loaded onto carts.

"Wait!" Van Helsing called after her. Then his attention was caught again by the enormous vampire creatures.

The vampire brides soared over the rooftops, swooping down to attack townspeople as they pursued Anna. Van Helsing was amazed by their strength, their fury, and their grotesque appearance. Each had a twenty-foot wingspan and a heavily muscled body. But it was their contorted, nearly human faces that were most disturbing. They mowed through the town like a pack of locusts.

One bride grabbed a full-grown man, lifting him off the ground as if he weighed no more than a baby. "No, Verona!" he begged.

"Be happy in the knowledge that your blood shall keep me beautiful," the dark-haired Verona said. She sank her teeth into his neck, then dropped him.

Another of the brides circled slowly overhead, her long, thick blond hair streaming out behind her. She

was obviously searching for the real quarry—Anna.

Van Helsing knew he had to put a stop to this devastation. He scanned the area for his crossbow, eventually spotting it under the feet of the trampling crowd. He grabbed it, took aim, and fired again and again and again. But each time Dracula's brides were simply too quick for him. He missed every single shot.

Now the town square was filled with weeping and howling in addition to terrified shouts.

"Carl!" Van Helsing shouted, hoping the little friar could hear him above the din. "I'm out of ammunition!"

Carl dashed forward with another round. Van Helsing reloaded and let loose arrow after arrow in rapid succession, spinning, twirling, turning as the brides swooped around the square, then soared high above the square again.

Anna popped back up from behind a crate. She eyed the dozens of deadly bolts sticking out of the boards she was hiding behind. "Who are you trying to kill?" she shouted at Van Helsing.

Van Helsing cleared his throat to shout out a response, but the square had gone dead quiet. The three terrifying bat-women had vanished.

He glanced back at Anna, who was climbing out of her hiding place. He gave her a questioning look.

"The sun," she said in answer to his unasked question.

A tiny sliver of sunlight had managed to break through the thick cloud cover.

A loud splash behind Van Helsing made him whip around. Something had dropped into the well. He and Anna both approached it cautiously.

The surreal silence was almost more frightening than the frenzy had been moments before. Van Helsing's brow furrowed. *Is it all over?* People glanced around nervously. Everyone in the square seemed to be collectively holding their breath. They were all wondering the same thing.

Still on alert, Van Helsing and Anna gazed down into the well. It was dark down there; they couldn't see a thing.

As they looked, it got even darker. The clouds had moved back over the sun once more.

Whoosh! Van Helsing's broad-brimmed hat blew off, swept away by the powerful rush of air that hit him when a red-haired vampire bat rocketed straight up out of the well. The creature grabbed Anna and rose high into the air.

Van Helsing tried to aim his crossbow at Aleera but Anna kept getting into the line of fire as she struggled in the vampire's grip.

He watched, amazed, as Anna reached down and pulled a switchblade from a strap on her boot. She flicked it open and jabbed it hard into the vampire's ankle. The creature howled in pain, then threw Anna into the air. Verona swooped in and caught her.

Van Helsing let loose a hail of steel bolts. Verona yowled in agony and dropped Anna as a lone arrow impaled her foot. Anna landed on a rooftop, then tumbled over the side.

Van Helsing couldn't worry about Anna's condition just yet. The third vampire bride, Marishka, was coming straight toward him. He shot the vampires again and again. She spiraled wildly across the square and crashed through the side of a building.

Van Helsing and Carl raced to the building, and as they reached the door it burst open. Marishka blasted out, arrows embedded in her chest and face. She slapped Van Helsing with such force that he went flying across the square.

Van Helsing gaped at her as he sprawled in the dirt. She yanked out the arrows and transformed into a young woman. Her wounds healed immediately.

But she was still very, very angry. She hissed and let her fangs drop down, then transformed back into the enormous white bat. She soared into the air, cackling like a deranged creature.

Carl leapt up and shouted, "This should do the trick." He threw a small vial of holy water to Van Helsing, but before Van Helsing could catch it, Verona swooped in and snatched it. She tossed the water into the well below her and flew off.

"Too bad. So sad," Marishka cooed. She flew over Van Helsing, knocking him to the ground. In a minute he was up again, wielding his crossbow and racing to the church in the village square. Marishka followed him, reaching the square just as Van Helsing dipped his arrows into a basin of holy water. Claws and fangs extended, she rocketed toward him.

Verona and Aleera, both transformed into creatures that looked like women, now had Anna trapped between them in a small pub off the village square. "Hello, Anna, my dear," hissed Verona as she moved in for the kill.

"You won't have me, Verona."

Verona smiled evilly and licked her lips. "The last of the Valeriouses," she murmured. Her canines distended into grisly pointed fangs. Just as she was about to bite down on Anna's neck, Anna punched her. Verona grabbed Anna's hand—quick as lightning— and forced her to the ground.

"I want first bite," Aleera announced, stepping up

to the two of them. Verona nodded consent and Aleera bared her fangs and bent toward Anna.

Before she could bite down, both brides turned back into great white bats and let out wild shrieks. "Marishka!" they screeched. A shock wave of wind blew Anna across the room as the bats flew overhead and out the windows, wailing insanely.

Back in the town square, Van Helsing fired at Marishka. Bolts from the weapon pounded into the vampire bride. Marishka shrieked horribly. Her flesh sizzled as she spiraled upward and slammed into the church spire. She hung there, pinned to the spire by the arrows in her chest.

The townspeople went silent as they all stared at the dying vampire. Van Helsing braced himself. He knew what he was about to witness—he had been here before. Sure enough, he watched the evil creature transform into a beautiful young woman—the girl she had been before she'd become a vampire.

Marishka glared down at Van Helsing, her green eyes filled with hate and pain. Then, with a last, inhuman hiss, she decayed into a molten mass of rotting flesh.

FOUR

Whispers filled the square all around Van Helsing. "He killed a bride." "He killed Marishka!" "He killed a vampire."

Funny, Van Helsing thought, watching the towns-people creep out of their hiding places. *You'd think they'd be a bit more grateful.*

"Vampire killer." A man shook a pitchfork at him.

"He killed one of them," a woman shouted, then spat on the ground.

"I don't get it," Carl said. "Isn't that a good thing?"

The man with the top hat stepped forward. Van Helsing disliked the scrawny fellow on sight. The man smiled an oily smile. "The vampires kill only what they need to survive. One or two people a month. But now . . ." He shook his head. "Now they will kill for revenge!"

This crowd is getting more dangerous by the minute, Van Helsing thought as villagers approached him with

pitchforks and machetes drawn. He scanned the square for the most useful escape route.

"Are you always this popular?" Carl asked.

Van Helsing shrugged. "Pretty much."

"And what name, my good sir, do I put on your gravestone?" the man in the top hat asked. He handed Van Helsing a card; UNDERTAKER was written across it.

Van Helsing saw Anna push her way through to the front of the crowd. He was relieved to see she was still alive. He had lost track of her during the melee, and he would not have forgiven himself if she'd been harmed.

"His name is Van Helsing," she announced.

A murmur washed over the crowd as they repeated his name to one another. Van Helsing noted how quickly the mood of the mob transformed from angry to admiring.

"Your reputation precedes you," Anna said. It was clear to Van Helsing that she admired him less than the crowd did.

"As does yours, Anna Valerious," Van Helsing said. From her expression he gathered that she hadn't known that he had recognized her as well. "And next time, stay close," he ordered. "You're no good to me dead."

Anna laughed. "Well, I'll say this for you: You've got courage." She hopped up on to the ledge of the

well to address the crowd. "Van Helsing is the first person to kill a vampire in one hundred years. I'd say that's earned him a drink!"

"Marishka!"

Icicles hung from the wooden rafters of the thirteenth-century fortress; stalagmites rose in spiky formations from the stone floor. In the center of the cavernous space stood a coffin made of ice and covered in snow.

Sobs punctuated the deep silence, echoing against the hard, sharp surfaces. The snow and ice melted into steam as Count Dracula rose up from his resting place, deeply saddened.

"Why can't they just leave us alone?" he moaned. "We never kill more than our share." He stalked across the frozen patches of his lair and up one of the massive frost-covered columns. As he passed the ancient candelabras suspended from the ceiling, the candles ignited.

He continued walking across the ceiling, his cape dangling from his shoulders as he made his way, upside down, toward his two remaining brides. They clung together, weeping, each hanging from the rafters by her feet.

"Aleera and Verona," he addressed them. "Did I

not say how important it was to finish with these Valeriouses?" he demanded. "We are so close to fulfilling our dream!"

The brides sobbed harder, wailing as if their hearts—if they had them—would break.

He waved a hand at them dismissively. "Ah, what's done is done. Or rather, what's not been done will be done all in good time. Now I must find out who our new visitor is."

He dropped down the forty feet to the floor. "Yes, we will make a special meal out of him. We are much too close to success to be interrupted now."

The two brides dropped down beside him. "No, my lord, please!" Aleera begged.

"My heart could not bear the sorrow if we fail again," Verona wailed.

"Silence!" Dracula boomed.

The brides cowered in fear. Dracula's demeanor changed instantly, and he pulled them close to him, wrapping them in his cape. "No, no, no," he crooned, as if he were comforting frightened children. "You must not fear me. Everyone else fears me."

The brides began to relax, and Dracula continued in a soothing, sing-song voice. "Perhaps you're right. We'll wait and see what to do about this stranger . . . and the woman."

"Now what shall we do?" Verona asked.

Dracula smiled. "We continue as planned. We will go to Castle Frankenstein!"

Anna Valerious led Van Helsing and Carl into the armory of her family castle. Van Helsing took in the four centuries of nasty-looking weaponry conveniently packed into a single room.

Carl was fascinated by all the weapons but Van Helsing was all business.

"Where do I find Dracula?" Van Helsing asked Anna.

"He used to live in this very house, four centuries ago," Anna explained. "No one knows where he lives now." She gestured to a large oil painting that covered an entire wall. It was a richly colored map, complete with fanciful—and frightening—mythological creatures decorating the borders. "Transylvania," Anna informed Carl and Van Helsing.

"My father would stare at that painting for hours. He seemed to think the map was the key to finding Dracula's lair."

Anna grabbed a sword, an iron mace, and some throwing stars. "So that's why you've come? To find Dracula?"

"I can help you," Van Helsing said.

"No one can help me," Anna replied.

"I can try," Van Helsing countered.

"You can die trying. Believe me, I know. My whole family has. Everyone but me. I can handle this myself."

Van Helsing smirked. "So I noticed."

Anna spun around, fury flashing in her dark eyes. "The vampires have never attacked in daylight before. I was unprepared. It won't happen again."

"Why did they attack in daylight?"

Anna thought for a moment. "They wanted to catch me off guard. They seem almost desperate to finish off my family."

"Why is that?" Van Helsing asked. "Why now?"

"You ask a lot of questions," Anna said.

"Usually I ask only two," Van Helsing replied. "The first one is, what are we dealing with, and the second is, how do I kill it?"

Anna strapped on a metal chest-plate and spiked gauntlets. "My father spent most of his life looking for the answer to those very questions. Year after year." She pointed out the window to the turreted north tower. "He tore apart that tower, combing through the family archives."

"Carl," Van Helsing said. "Stop admiring the toys and check out the tower."

"Right." Carl nodded, then picked up an ivory-plated rifle.

"Carl?" Van Helsing said.

"Yes?" Carl turned and looked at Van Helsing. He put down the rifle. "Right, the tower. Now."

Carl bustled out of the room. Anna strapped on a scabbard and headed for the sword collection. Van Helsing stepped in front of her. "The only way to save your family is to stay alive until Dracula is killed."

"And who will kill him if not me?" Anna demanded. "Who will show courage if not me?"

"If you go out there alone, you'll be outmanned and outpositioned." He gestured toward the window. "Besides, you can't see in the dark. In the morning," Van Helsing assured her, "we'll hunt him together."

Anna gave him a long look. "Thank you," she said. "But I'm going now."

She pushed past him and grabbed one of the swords from the wall. She shoved it into the scabbard.

Van Helsing watched her continue to make her preparations for battle. "I'm sorry you have to carry this burden," he said.

"I wouldn't have it any other way," Anna countered.

She grabbed a helmet and lowered it over her face. *She is every inch a warrior*, Van Helsing thought with admiration.

"And I'm sorry about your father and your brother," he said.

"I will see them again, when we have opened the way to heaven." Anna faced him squarely, her eyes glittering with fierce courage from behind the helmet.

As Anna passed Van Helsing, he grabbed her arm and spun her around. Before she could react he blew a fine blue powder into her beautiful face. She blinked, her eyes wide with surprise inside her helmet, then sank to the floor.

Van Helsing stood over her, gazing down at her limp form. "And I'm sorry about that too."

FIVE

A nna woke slowly, trying to piece together what had happened. She was in her bedroom. "How did I get in here?" she murmured sleepily. She was still wearing her clothes, but her armor had all been removed. She felt very groggy.

She sat bolt upright in bed. It all came back to her in a rush of clarity. "Van Helsing!" She shouted as many Romanian curses as she could think of as she clambered out of bed. She called Van Helsing every terrible name she had ever heard, and then she made up a few of her own.

She stormed out of her room, ready to knock that self-important braggart on his overconfident butt. "I'll show him he can't just—"

A creaking sound stopped her. She had arrived at the door to the armory. She froze, then realized it was probably Van Helsing inside arming himself. She

smiled. Now she could curse him and all of his descendants in person.

She flung open the door to the armory. "Van Helsing?" she called.

There was another creak, this time from somewhere among the long rows of weapons. She moved farther into the room.

The skin on the back of her neck prickled. *I'm being watched*, she realized. All of her senses went on alert. Her eyes scanned the gloom, but she couldn't see anything.

She grabbed a flickering lantern from one of the sconces and walked along the cases of weapons. *Why doesn't Van Helsing reveal himself?* she wondered. *Is he spying on me? Or is he hiding so that I don't catch him in here?*

Another creak made her jump, and her cheeks flushed. She hoped Van Helsing hadn't noticed that! She came around a corner and discovered an open window. Its shutter creaked as it swayed in the wind and rain.

Anna let out a sigh of relief. She wasn't in danger, and, even better, that arrogant Van Helsing hadn't witnessed her little display of nerves. She crossed to close the window when the light of the full moon illuminated something strange on the floor. She knelt

down, and her forehead furrowed in confusion.

"Paw prints," she murmured, her heart pounding faster. She held up the lantern to try to see where the large prints led. They stopped mysteriously in the center of the armory.

She stood back up and grabbed a mace from the wall. Moving slowly, she followed the paw prints, then stopped. She looked up and down the rows. Empty. Then she heard a low growl, and her breath caught. Where had the sound come from?

A drop of rainwater splashed down onto her cheek. Her head whipped straight up and she saw it. A werewolf, its fur dripping from the rain, dangled from the beam above her.

The werewolf let out a roar and dropped to the ground. Anna flung her lantern at it, then turned and ran as fast as she could. She raced back among the weapons cases, dashing through the maze of swords, spears, guns, and armor. The exit seemed so far away! She careened around a case holding cannon ammunition and slammed right into someone. She cocked back her arm, ready to use her mace, but the person grabbed her wrist.

It was her beloved brother.

"Velkan?" she gasped. "You're alive!" She threw herself into his arms. "Oh, Velkan!"

"Quiet, Anna," Velkan said. "I only have a moment."

"Velkan, we must get out of here." Anna gripped his hand and tried to drag him toward the door. "There's a werewolf—"

Velkan cut her off. "Never mind that. Listen to me. I know Dracula's secret! He has *mumblich nowger lochen . . .*"

Anna stared at Velkan. His eyes went round and he seemed to be having trouble controlling his words, his mouth.

"What is it?" Anna asked. "What's wrong?"

But he couldn't answer.

Anna watched in horror as Velkan's body spasmed and jerked. He lurched and stumbled toward the window where Anna could see the clouds roll away to reveal a full moon. Velkan twisted his tormented body around to face Anna. "Run! Anna, run!"

But Anna was frozen in place, staring at her brother. He tore at his clothing, ripping it to shreds as his hands enlarged and curved into claws. Howling as if he were in great pain, Velkan shuddered and contorted and clawed at his flesh.

Anna couldn't tear her eyes away from the gruesome sight of her brother transforming into a werewolf—powerful, brutish, and clearly vicious. He threw

back his head, opened his fang-filled mouth, and bayed at the full moon.

The door behind Anna burst open, but she was too stunned to move. "Anna!" Van Helsing exclaimed.

The werewolf howled again, then threw itself through the balcony doors. Shattered glass rained down around Anna as she stared numbly into the rainy night.

Van Helsing ran up to her. "Are you all right?" he demanded.

Anna couldn't respond. *My brother didn't die*, she realized. *He has been turned into that loathsome creature.* It took every ounce of control she had to not dissolve into tears. She knew that crying would not help—her or her brother.

Van Helsing raced out onto the balcony and peered down. "He got away," he reported.

The door opened again, and Carl stumbled in. "Why does it smell like wet dog in here?" he asked.

"Werewolf," Van Helsing replied.

"Ah. Right. You'll be needing silver bullets then."

Carl scrounged around in his robe and pulled out a bandolier filled with gleaming silver bullets. He tossed it to Van Helsing, who caught it and slung it over his shoulder. He strode to the door, Carl following close behind him.

Anna snapped out of her shock and ran after Van Helsing. "No, wait!" she cried.

Van Helsing slammed the door shut behind him. Anna tried opening it, but it was no use. It was jammed shut from the outside. Anna pounded on the door, furious. "Van Helsing!"

I can't believe this, she thought. Angered by Van Helsing's behavior and drained by what she'd seen, Anna slid down the door and slumped on the floor.

Van Helsing stalked the labyrinthine streets of the village, hunting for his quarry. All was quiet at this time of night, the only sound the muffled revelry coming from the pubs. Some instinct told him to stop. He stood for a moment, scanned the darkness, then inhaled deeply.

"Wet dog," he murmured, recognizing the scent.

A flash of fur exploded out of a distant alley. Van Helsing fired his gun filled with silver bullets. In a blur of incredible speed, the beast dodged back and forth across the street. It raced from doorway to doorway, getting closer, always one step ahead of Van Helsing's shots. It vanished into an alley twenty feet in front of him.

Who is hunting whom? Van Helsing wondered as he backed up.

He raised his gun, ready to pump the werewolf full of silver bullets.

"No!" Anna came out of nowhere and appeared at Van Helsing's side. She knocked his arm holding the gun, sending the shot wild and blasting out the gas streetlight.

The werewolf took advantage of the momentary confusion to dash out of its hiding place and vanish around a corner. Furious, Van Helsing charged after it, just in time to see the werewolf dart into the dark forest.

Anna ran up beside him. Van Helsing whirled around, grabbed her, and shoved her against the wall.

"Why did you interfere?" he demanded. "I had the werewolf in my sights!"

Anna's hands gripped his fingers that were wrapped around her throat. "I— You're choking me," she gasped.

Van Helsing loosened his grip but only a little. "Give me a reason not to," he snarled.

Anna's eyes were wide with terror. "I—I can't," she said. "If people knew . . ."

Van Helsing stared down at her for a moment, then released her. Her hands flew to her throat, rubbing her neck, sore from Van Helsing's rough grip.

"He's not your brother anymore," Van Helsing said.

Anna stared at him. "You knew?"

Van Helsing nodded. "I guessed."

Anna's jaw tightened. "You guessed before or after I stopped you from shooting him?"

"Before," Van Helsing admitted.

"And you still tried to kill him?" Anna demanded.

"He's a werewolf," Van Helsing replied evenly. "He's going to kill people."

"It's not his fault! He can't help it!"

"I know. But he has to be stopped."

Anna stared down at the ground. "They say Dracula has a cure," she said. She lifted her gaze to meet Van Helsing's. He saw pleading and fury there. "If there's a chance I can save my brother, I'm going after it." She turned to leave, but Van Helsing grabbed her arm.

"I'm here to find Dracula," he reminded her. "And that's all."

"And I need to find my brother! He gave his life for me. He's the only family I have left!" All of the fiery defiance drained out of her, and she slumped against the wall. "I despise Dracula more than you can ever imagine," she said sadly. "He has taken everything from me. He has left me all alone in the world."

Van Helsing gazed at her sympathetically. He

began to understand what drove this intense and gorgeous woman. He stroked her cheek lightly and lifted her chin with his finger. "To have memories of those you have loved and lost is perhaps harder than to have no memories at all."

Anna turned her head away, blinking back tears. It was clear to Van Helsing that any further kindness from him might make her lose the very shaky control she had over her emotions. He knew she needed to be allowed to stay strong. He sighed and ran his hands through his long dark hair. He made a decision he hoped he wouldn't regret.

"Okay," he said. "Let's go find your brother."

SIX

Castle Frankenstein perched high on its cliff, strangled by a thick mesh of vines and brambles. The sky swirled with dense clouds as lightning flashed and thunder rumbled.

Inside the abandoned laboratory, little creatures known as Dwergi worked feverishly, doing Dracula's bidding. The short, squat Dwergi wore enormous goggles, giving them an insect-like appearance. Their flat faces seemed almost mummified, and the spiky metal breastplates they sported looked lethal.

A Dwerger slammed down a switch, and the dark lab sparked into life. As the massive dynamos, generators, gears, and fan belts kicked in, brilliant arcs of electricity shot up and down the coils of wire. The little Dwergi swarmed around the equipment, preparing for the task ahead.

A crash of thunder and a blinding lightning bolt brought Dracula to the window. *The storm is reaching*

its peak, he noted. "Soon," he murmured. "It must be soon." He turned back into the room. "Igor!" he shouted up to the rafters.

Igor gazed down from the skylight, rain lashing his twisted body, heavy wind practically blowing him off his feet. His long pale hair dripped with rain.

"Yes, master?" Igor shouted back above the wild storm.

"Have you finished?" Dracula demanded.

"Yes! All is done! We're coming down to make the final attachments."

"Good!" Dracula shouted up to his servant. "Good," he repeated, rubbing his hands together. *All is going according to plan. This time success may be within my reach.*

A werewolf slipped in through a break in the granite wall, but Dracula ignored it. It was no threat to the count, and its presence was a necessary irritant.

"Werewolves are such a nuisance during their first full moon," Dracula commented. "They're so hard to control."

The werewolf continued to stare at Dracula as it transformed back into Velkan, the once proud and handsome prince of the gypsies.

Dracula continued to check the equipment, tightening a bolt here, twisting a wire there. "I sent you on

a simple task," Dracula complained. "It was your assignment to find out who our new friend is, and what do you do? You stop to have a little chat with your cursed sister."

"Leave her out of it," Velkan snapped. "She doesn't know your secret. And I am soon to take it to my grave."

Dracula stepped up to a filthy iron pod, form-fitted for a huge human body. A burned corpse lay inside of it.

"Don't wish for death so quickly, my friend," Dracula warned. "I intend for you to be useful."

"I would rather die than help you," Velkan vowed.

"Oh, don't be so predictable," Dracula sneered. "You know, everyone who has ever said that does indeed die." Dracula unfastened the metal straps holding the corpse in place. "Besides, tonight after the final stroke of midnight, you'll have no choice but to obey me."

He lifted the corpse from the pod and dumped it at Velkan's feet. "Look familiar?" Dracula asked.

Velkan stepped backward, then gazed at the pathetic and ruined body on the floor in front of him. "Father?" he gasped, his voice breaking.

Dracula lunged for Velkan, lifted him off his feet, and slammed him down in the pod. Igor instantly

barked orders to the Dwergi, and the little creatures hurried to strap Velkan into the pod.

"Your father proved useless to our cause," Dracula told Velkan. "I'm hoping with werewolf venom running through your veins, you will be of greater benefit."

Dracula grabbed a rusty metal helmet and shoved it onto Velkan's head. He quickly attached the wires and electrodes sticking out of the helmet to the generators. Velkan struggled against the straps and writhed so vigorously that it took six Dwergi and Igor to hold him in place long enough for Dracula to do the fitting.

Finally Velkan stopped struggling. "I may have failed to kill you, Count," Velkan threatened. "But my sister will not."

Van Helsing and Anna trotted their horses along a snowy country lane. The sky above them swirled with dark clouds, the silent night interrupted by crashing thunder and the sound of their horses' hooves.

They had left Carl in Castle Valerious searching for clues to Dracula's whereabouts. Van Helsing didn't mention his own detour to search for Anna's brother. He didn't want the young friar to feel compromised by this deviation from the assigned mission.

Van Helsing and Anna had been able to follow the large paw prints the werewolf had left in the muddy road leading out of town. Now their eyes constantly scanned the forest on either side of them.

"What's that?" Van Helsing asked, nodding toward something in their path up ahead.

They halted their horses and dismounted. Anna dashed ahead and lifted up strands of long coarse hair. "Werewolves shed only before their first full moon," she informed Van Helsing. "He must be nearby."

"Up there, maybe." Van Helsing gazed up at the castle looming above them. Spectacular arcs of electricity flashed out of the tower windows. "Someone's up there creating that light show."

Anna stared up at the ominous castle. "That's strange. The castle is supposed to be deserted," she commented. "A Dr. Frankenstein lived here until about a year ago. He was a grave robber. The rumor was that he had used the bodies to create a monster. He was killed."

"A year ago," Van Helsing repeated. "That's when your father went missing, isn't it?"

"Yes, just after that." She headed for the shattered front gate.

Van Helsing dashed forward and spun her around so that she faced the tangled shrubbery. "There are

those who go through the front door, and there are those who get to live just a little bit longer."

Anna's eyes widened as he pointed to the strange shapes in the briars and brambles. "Skeletons," Van Helsing said. "And decaying corpses. They aren't exactly a welcoming sight."

Anna nodded silently.

"Why don't we try a side entrance," Van Helsing suggested. "I'd like to avoid becoming part of this gruesome landscape, wouldn't you?"

SEVEN

Van Helsing and Anna crept through the gloomy castle halls, weapons at the ready. They had tied their horses in a secluded wooded area, not too far from the main road. Everywhere around them Van Helsing noticed the telltale signs of some kind of violent event. It wasn't just the obvious collection of dead bodies outside, but also the smashed doors, splintered battering rams, and walls and trees blackened from fire.

Something terrible happened here a year ago, he surmised. *And then a new horror began.* He kept his observations to himself, however. He figured Anna could put two and two together. Besides, he didn't want to point out to her that the more recent devastation could be directly related to her brother's transformation into a werewolf.

Van Helsing and Anna continued wordlessly through the cavernous castle halls. Brackish water

covered the floor, supporting Van Helsing's conclusion that no one had lived in the castle for some time. No one human, that is.

Suddenly, a small creature wearing large round goggles dashed across the hall ahead of them, vanishing into another corridor.

Van Helsing raised his rifle into position at his shoulder.

Anna pushed his gun to aim lower down. "Dwerger," she commented.

"Huh?" Van Helsing raised an eyebrow.

"One of Dracula's servants," Anna explained. "They are about hip-height. If you get the chance to kill one, do it. They'll do worse to you."

"Right."

Another Dwerger scurried up ahead, shouting orders in Romanian. Van Helsing quickly lowered his rifle to hip height, adjusting to the small stature of the creature. It was obviously not human, though what it was precisely, he couldn't guess.

Anna grew pale beside Van Helsing. "They're using my brother for some sort of experiment," she gasped. "We have to save him," Anna insisted.

"Anna." Van Helsing turned to face her.

"My brother is still battling the sickness within him. There is still hope!"

"Anna!" Van Helsing was more stern this time. He had to make her understand. "There is no hope for your brother. But we can still protect others by killing Dracula."

Anna's shoulders slumped, and Van Helsing could see the sorrow and defeat on her beautiful face.

Staying close to the walls, they entered what once had been an enormous foyer. Van Helsing's face wrinkled with disgust. Hanging from the ceiling, rafters, and beams were hundreds of gooey white sacs. The lumpy, bulbous things were about the size of watermelons.

"Have you ever seen these before?" he whispered to Anna.

She looked as if she was going to gag. She shook her head. "What do you think they are?"

Van Helsing stepped up to one of the sacs to examine it more closely. His eyes widened as the answer came to him. "Cocoons," he said. "These must contain the offspring of Dracula and his brides."

"No!" Anna exclaimed. She came to stand beside Van Helsing and peered at the cocoon. "Of course," she finally said. "Vampires are the walking dead. It makes sense that their children are born dead."

Van Helsing spotted something sticking into the cocoon. A copper wire. *Come to think of it*, he noted,

there are wires inserted into all the cocoons. "Dracula must be trying to find a way to bring them to life using electrical power." He began to load his rifle with his silver nitrate shells. "I was told that Dracula and his brides kill only one or two people a month. If they bring all of these monstrosities to life . . ."

He looked at Anna, and the expression of horror on her face told him she understood his implication.

Lightning flashed, illuminating the cocoons momentarily. The copper wires buzzed and crackled with electrical energy. The cocoons writhed as the current pulsed into them.

"Agh!" Van Helsing jumped back, startled, as a head burst out of the cocoon in front of him.

The creature was some kind of bat, but it had a humanoid face. Its huge, lidless eyeballs were covered in veins, and a hairy pig snout sat in the middle of its mottled greenish skin. It let out a shriek, revealing a mouth full of razor-sharp teeth.

Anna shrieked, and stumbled backward, bumping into Van Helsing. He clapped a hand over her mouth and dragged her deeper into the shadows. A movement on the balcony across the grand foyer had told him they were not alone with the cocoons anymore. Dracula and his two remaining brides, Verona and Aleera, were leaning on the balcony, surveying the scene below them.

As the storm worsened, lights flashed all around the room. Sparks flew, wires buzzed, and all of the cocoons pulsated madly. Van Helsing could feel Anna trembling, though he couldn't tell if it was in fear or outrage. The rhythm of the electrical output crescendoed until suddenly all of the cocoons burst open at once. The vampire offspring exploded out, shrieking and flying around the foyer.

The brides leapt from the balcony, transforming into bats, their long elegant gowns becoming wings. They swooped around the room to romp with their chittering offspring. The horrible sound was deafening.

Dracula smiled with satisfaction, then pointed to the window. "You must feed!" he shouted over the din of chirps and squeaks and shrieks. "To the village! All of you!"

"This is where I come in," Van Helsing whispered.

"No! Wait! You can't!" Anna protested. He ignored her and stepped out into the room. He opened fire, pumping silver nitrate bullets into the hideous things. With every hit, a vampire offspring exploded, bursting into black goo.

Dracula screamed in outrage and leapt from the balcony. His cape fluttered behind him, then transformed into enormous black wings.

Van Helsing slammed his gun back into his holster and sprinted out of the foyer, grabbing Anna's hand along the way. He could feel the wind created by the great vampire's enormous bat wings behind them.

"We should split up," Van Helsing panted. "He can only chase one of us."

"Got it!" Anna took a sharp turn and ran up a flight of stone stairs.

Van Helsing clambered up onto a side table, found hand and footholds in the rough stone wall, and pulled himself up into the rafters. Balancing himself on the thick wooden beam, he forced himself to breathe quietly.

And waited.

EIGHT

Anna dashed up the stone stairs two at a time. She wasn't crazy about the idea of Van Helsing using himself as a decoy, or of getting lost in this castle on her own, but she knew it was the right move. Besides, she had a plan and she didn't think Van Helsing would approve.

She raced up the stairs to the very top. Then she wandered the pitch-black halls until she found the door she was looking for. *Yes*, she thought. *This should lead into the tower room where I saw those lights. The laboratory where they are keeping my brother. And where I shall free him.*

She pulled her saber from its scabbard and gripped it tightly, then tugged open the door inch by inch until she could slip inside. She was in luck; mayhem ruled the day in the laboratory. Wires were short-circuiting, and the squat little Dwergi were frantically manipulating controls and levers.

"Igor!" a Dwerger shouted to the misshapen man prowling the room. "We're almost up to maximum!"

"We're losing power!" Igor cried over the crashing thunder. "The human is insufficient."

Another clap of thunder, another crack of lightning. Anna's eyes were slow to adjust to the constantly shifting light levels. First she was blinded by the sparks and sudden lightning, then she was plunged into darkness again. Between the bursts of lightning the room was illuminated only by the glowing and humming wires.

"Accelerate the generator!" Igor screamed as he paced the laboratory. "Power the dynamos!"

Anna crept deeper into the room, taking care to stay low, so as not to be seen over the worktables. As she approached the center of the lab, she realized she was being rained on. She glanced up and saw an iron pod on a scaffold raised high above the floor, right under the shattered skylight. All of the wires emanated from whatever was in that iron pod.

Another bolt of lightning struck, hitting the pod. *Is it some kind of lightning rod?* Anna wondered. *No, those are used to protect a house from the electric current.*

Then she understood: These creatures were using the energy from the electrical storm to power all of the

machinery in the lab. This same energy was being channeled into Dracula's offspring: This was how he was trying to bring them to life. And whatever was on that pod above her was acting as the electricity's conductor.

Another crash of lightning and thunder rattled the pod violently. An arm flopped over the side of the pod.

Anna gasped, recognizing the jacket sleeve. "Velkan." The horror of how he was being used sickened her, but there was no time for emotion now. *I must save him*, she vowed. *But how?*

Van Helsing peered down from his hiding place up near the ceiling. Dracula had returned to his undead human form, his wings a cape again. He walked along the stone corridor and came to a stop just under Van Helsing.

"I can tell the character of a man by the sound of his heartbeat," Dracula said matter-of-factly. He cocked his head as if he were listening. "Strange that yours is so steady."

Does he really know where I am? Van Helsing wondered. *Well, no sense in waiting to find out. It's now or never.*

Van Helsing gripped his wooden stake, took a

deep breath, and dropped down directly onto the count. As Dracula stumbled under the sudden, surprising weight, Van Helsing plunged the stake deep into the vampire's chest. He gave it a good twist to be sure it stayed put and then stepped back.

An enormous sense of relief flooded through him. It was all over. Even better—killing Dracula would destroy all the creatures he had sired: the brides and the grotesque multitude of offspring. *Mission accomplished*, he thought with satisfaction.

Dracula stared down at the weapon sticking out of his chest, then back up at Van Helsing. Van Helsing's skin crawled as Dracula gave him a calm smile and said, "Hello, Van Helsing."

Huh? Van Helsing couldn't understand what was happening. *How can he know my name?* he wondered. *More importantly, why hasn't he turned into dust?*

Van Helsing stared unbelieving as Dracula casually wrapped his long, pale fingers around the hilt of the stake and pulled it out of his chest. The Count released it, letting it clatter to the floor.

A slow smile spread across Dracula's unnaturally handsome face. "You don't remember, do you?"

Van Helsing forced his expression to stay neutral, but his mind was racing. *That stake should have worked!*

Why didn't it work? He stood his ground, playing for time, hoping that he'd come up with some idea of how to kill this creature. "What exactly am I supposed to remember?"

Dracula shook his head almost sadly. "You are the great Van Helsing. Trained by monks and mullahs from Tibet to Istanbul. Protected by Rome herself. But like me, you are hunted by all others."

Van Helsing shrugged. "The Order knows all about you, so I guess it's no surprise that you know all about me."

Dracula waggled a finger at him, almost playfully. "Oh, but it's much more than that. You and I go back a long way, Gabriel."

Van Helsing could feel his heart thudding a little harder. Something about Dracula's manner and the turn of the conversation made him uncomfortable.

"I know why you have such horrific nightmares," Dracula said. "The horrible scenes of ancient battles past. Oh, and those triangular scars on your back. Do you know how you received them?" He paused for a moment, obviously relishing the game he was playing with Van Helsing.

Van Helsing's eyes narrowed. "How do you know me?"

* * *

Anna crept across the metal scaffolding and headed for her brother. She was soaked to the skin from the rain pummeling her, but still she kept at it. She ignored the shrill cries of Dracula's offspring as they swarmed around the castle heading for town.

She reached her brother and began unstrapping the belts holding him down. "Oh, Velkan, what have they done to you?"

At the sound of her voice, Velkan's head whipped in her direction. Gradually his eyes filled with clarity and Anna could see that the delirium had passed. He recognized her. Or maybe seeing her cut through the agony, recalling him to who he truly was. But for some reason, instead of seeming relieved that she was here helping him to escape, he began frantically pushing at her with his free arm.

"Don't, Velkan," she whispered. "It's all right. I've come to save you."

The clock in one of the castle's towers began chiming. *Good,* Anna thought, as she continued to struggle with her frantic brother. *Those bells will help drown out any sounds we're making up here.* The wet leather straps were difficult to undo. She continued working the buckles as the clock chimed ten . . . eleven . . . twelve.

Midnight.

Velkan reached out and gripped Anna's arm. Her eyes widened as his fingers transformed into powerful claws and his flesh seemed to melt away. He was becoming a werewolf!

She let out a shriek and struggled in his clutches.

Van Helsing's eyes flicked up toward Anna's scream. But with Dracula standing right in front of him, he was trapped. If he ran up the stairs, Dracula would just follow him and Anna would be no safer. Besides, Dracula was his true quarry. How could he leave the count to go rescue Anna?

Dracula behaved as if he had heard nothing. "So, would you like me to refresh your memory? Give you a few details from your sordid past?"

Van Helsing reached inside his cloak and yanked out a large crucifix, thrusting it toward Dracula. Dracula recoiled, stumbling backward several steps. But he quickly recovered.

Why aren't my usual weapons working? Van Helsing wondered. He could see that the crucifix affected the count a bit but not enough to do any damage.

Dracula fiddled with his cloak, regaining his composure. "I guess that's a conversation for another time," Dracula said. "But before you go, let me reintroduce

Van Helsing—legendary monster hunter

Carl shows Van Helsing the latest in anti-monster technology.

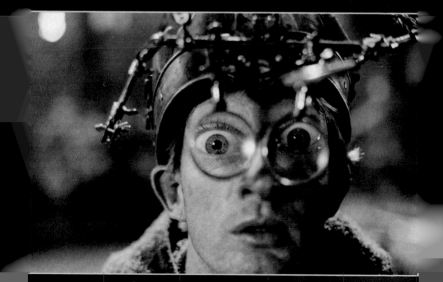

Carl finds out he's goi[ng]... [H]elsing to Transylvania.

Count Dracula needs Dr. Frankenstein's monster for his evil plan.

Dr. Frankenstein is ready to bring his creation to life.

Princess Anna, the last of the Valerious family

Anna and Van Helsing team up.

The cross has no effect on Count Dracula.

A Dwerger is ready to do Count
Dracula's bidding.

The Brides of Dracula take flight.

The Wolf Man attacks.

The count throws a deadly masked ball.

Frankenstein's monster

Mayhem at Castle Dracula

myself." He bowed theatrically. "Count Vladislaus Dragulia. Born 1432. Murdered 1462." He smiled at Van Helsing again, and his bicuspids descended into lethal-looking fangs.

Van Helsing backed up, immediately assessing possible escape routes, since clearly his weapons were useless. Running away was the only choice. He needed to rethink his strategy, and he had to stay alive long enough to do so. Forcing himself to ignore Anna's shouts, his eyes flicked around the corridor, while staying highly aware of Dracula's every breath.

I'll pass right into striking distance if I head for the stairs, Van Helsing noted. A dumbwaiter that had once brought food up from the kitchens below was just a few short feet away. It could serve him right now.

He faced the count, not wanting to betray a hint of his game plan. Dracula's eyes bored deeply into his. Then an eerie wailing sound filled the castle, drowning out even Anna's screams. Dracula startled and his gaze abruptly broke off. "My brides!" he cried.

In the one moment Dracula was distracted, Van Helsing leapt into the nearby dumbwaiter. Using one of his rotating saw blades, he cut through a cable, rocketing himself straight up the narrow shaft.

He shot up to the top floor, somersaulted out of

the dumbwaiter, then raced toward Anna's screams. He charged into the laboratory to see Anna wrestling with a werewolf. She yanked herself free and stumbled backward into Van Helsing. Startled, she let out another shriek as she whirled around. Van Helsing could see her relief when she realized that she had banged into a friend and not another foe.

"I think we've overstayed our welcome," Van Helsing quipped. He pulled a squat gun out of a holster and aimed it at a thick tree across the castle moat. *Thwack!* A cable shot out of the grappling gun and embedded itself into the tree with its knife-like point.

"Much quicker than taking the stairs." Van Helsing boosted Anna to the tether, and together they slid down along the cable.

"*Graaawh!*" The werewolf let out a furious howl and broke free of its restraints. It bounded to the edge of the scaffolding and slashed at the lifeline, snapping the cable. But the creature had missed its chance: Anna and Van Helsing swung out over the moat and landed safely at the edge of the dark forest on the other side.

They hit the ground running. "No time to rest," Anna panted.

"No kidding." Van Helsing and Anna raced away

from the castle. "Whoa! Watch out!" he cried as he leapt over the dead body of one of the vampire offspring. The gruesome creatures were littered all over the grounds.

"They're all dead!" Anna gasped.

"That was why the brides started wailing," Van Helsing said.

"What about our horses?" Anna asked.

"We'll get them later. If we're being watched, we don't want anyone to realize where we're really heading anyway. What we want is to get out of sight."

They darted through the forest until finally the trees thinned and they could slow down. Rain pelted the pair as they staggered their way across the dark moors. Anna scolded Van Helsing the entire time.

"A wooden stake?" she scoffed. "A silver crucifix? What did you think? That we hadn't already tried the obvious?"

"I—" Van Helsing began.

Anna cut him off. "We've been hunting this creature for more than four hundred years. We've shot him, stabbed him, clubbed him, doused him with holy water, and staked him in the heart, and still he lives!"

They'd reached an abandoned windmill, and Anna dashed for shelter under the charred remains of its sails. She glared at Van Helsing as he huddled beside

her. "Do you understand?" she demanded. "*Nobody* knows how to kill Dracula."

A slight smile creased Van Helsing's lips. "I could have used that information a little earlier."

Anna leaned against the windmill and lowered herself to the ground. Van Helsing watched all the fire drain out of her. She hugged her knees to her chest and let her long wet hair fall in front of her face. "You were right," she said softly. "He isn't my brother anymore. I should have allowed you to kill him when you wanted to."

Van Helsing knelt down beside her. "I'm sorry" was all he could think to say.

She nodded, then pushed her thick dark hair behind her ears. "What do you think killed the offspring?"

Van Helsing shrugged. "I'm not sure. I think maybe whatever they were using to power them wasn't strong enough."

Anna blinked back tears. "That's what they were trying to use my brother to do." She met Van Helsing's eyes directly. Her expression was soft, sad. "Do you have any family?" she asked.

"I'm not sure," he replied. "I hope to find out someday. That's what keeps me going."

"That must be hard," Anna said.

Van Helsing stood and tried to wring some of the rain from his clothing. *Useless*, he decided. Besides, they would have to go back out into that pelting storm again soon enough. "I wonder how Carl is making out back at your family fortress," he said.

Anna sighed and stood, too. "I guess we should retrieve the horses and head back there."

She stamped her feet as Van Helsing patted himself down, trying to warm up and get his circulation going. He could hear Anna muttering under her breath.

Good, he decided. *Better for her to be angry than sad. It will allow her to stay strong.*

Her muttering grew louder. "I hate that this is happening!" she shouted. She picked up a rock and hurled it at the ruined windmill.

"Feel better?" Van Helsing asked.

Anna smirked. "As a matter of fact, yes, I do."

"In that case . . ." Van Helsing grabbed a thick branch and threw it at the fire-damaged wall. He grinned at Anna. "You're right. That did make me feel better."

Laughing almost hysterically, they flung rocks and tree branches downed by the storm at the old windmill. Suddenly, they heard a loud creaking sound, and before their astonished eyes, the badly

damaged wall caved in, taking a large part of the earth with it.

"No!" Anna shrieked as she and Van Helsing fell through the soggy hole in the ground. They landed with a thud in an underground cavern.

NINE

Carl peeked out from underneath a large canopy bed, shaking with fear. *Those terrible creatures! Where did they come from?*

He had watched in horror from the tower window as hundreds of vicious little bat-vampires had darkened the sky. Dracula's brides, Verona and Aleera, had been with them on their rampage through the village, he was sure of it.

So Carl did the only sensible thing he could think to do: He scooted under the bed. From his hiding place, he had listened to the human screams and the awful screeching sound of the evil vermin. All the cries were mixed in with the rumbling thunder and torrential rain that seemed to be the usual weather in this accursed place. He longed for the sunny Mediterranean weather back in Rome and tried to calm himself by imagining he was reading a book on a sunny portico.

An eerie silence interrupted his thoughts.

It had been quiet for some time, now, he realized. He decided it would be safe to risk emerging.

He crept out from under the bed and knelt at the window. He pulled himself up just high enough to peer over the sill. It was still raining, but the sky had lightened, now that it was emptied of the nasty creatures. *No more flying monsters. Coast is clear.* He frowned, wondering what had happened to them. Then he shrugged. "Who cares?" he declared. "They're gone and that's what matters."

But now what should he do? He had no idea where Anna and Van Helsing were. Or if they were even still alive.

Carl sat on the floor, leaning against the wall. "Think," he ordered himself, tapping the back of his head lightly against the rough stones. "Think, think—whoa!" On the third tap, a panel in the wall beside him slid open. He turned to see an extraordinary painting of two medieval knights facing each other atop a cliff.

He stood to study it more carefully. *Whoever painted this made it look so real,* he thought. The sea churned below the knights, and the sky looked as if it was about to storm. A Latin inscription encircled the two fighting men. He translated it aloud:

"'Even a man who is pure in heart and says his

prayers by night may become a wolf when the wolf-bane blooms and the moon is shining bright,'" Carl read. "'Or crave another's blood when the sun goes down and his body takes to flight.'"

He scratched his head and bit his lip, considering the meaning of the inscription. "Well, that's not very reassuring, is it?"

Hang on, what's happening now? As Carl stared at the painting it seemed to come to life! The trees swayed in the powerful wind. Huge waves pounded the cliff, and the clock on the church tower began to chime. His mouth dropped open. The fighting knights transformed in front of his astounded eyes: one into a werewolf, and the other into a vampire! Snarling and hissing, the two evil creatures grappled with each other viciously.

"No!" he gasped, stumbling backward. He tripped over the bedclothes and sprawled flat on his face. Scrambling back up to his feet, he discovered the painting was just a painting again.

He sank onto the bed and used one of the sheets to mop his sweating brow. "I can't have seen what I thought I saw," he muttered. "Must be all the stress."

"Why are we going this way?" Anna asked. She and Van Helsing carefully made their way beside a

muddy trickling stream. The cavern was quite dim; the only light provided by tiny cracks in the roof that allowed in the weak moonlight. Bones crunched beneath their feet, and slimy, soggy vines dangled in their faces.

"The smell is horrible," Anna complained. "And it's getting worse heading in this direction."

"Exactly," Van Helsing replied. "That means we're on the right track."

Anna scowled at him, but kept going.

"Something has been living down here," Van Helsing said. He pointed to a massive pile of rat bones picked clean. "I think it's carnivorous and probably of human ancestry."

He knelt down and studied a pair of large muddy boot prints. "I'd say he's a size seventeen wide, about three hundred and sixty pounds, eight and a half to nine feet tall. He has a bad limp in his right leg." He looked back up to Anna. Then up and up and up. "And he has three copper teeth."

Anna smirked. "How do you know he has copper teeth?"

"Because he's standing right behind you." Van Helsing leapt to his feet and grabbed for his gun.

Anna whirled around. "The Frankenstein monster!" she gasped.

"Monster?" the creature thundered in a horrible, guttural rasp. "Who is the monster here?" He thudded forward, first one huge foot, then the other. "I have done nothing wrong, and yet you and all your kind wish me dead!"

Van Helsing flew into Frankenstein with all the force he could muster, slamming the monster's head against the rock wall. To his astonishment, the glass top of Frankenstein's head popped open.

With an annoyed growl, Frankenstein slammed the top of his head back down as if it were the lid on a box. He turned to go after Anna.

"What do you want?" Anna demanded.

"To exist!"

Taking advantage of Frankenstein's attention on Anna, Van Helsing quickly pulled a slim ivory blowgun from his inside coat pocket and loaded it with darts. Then he blew six darts right into the monster's back.

The creature howled and flailed, trying to swat the darts free. He lumbered unsteadily over the uneven cavern floor, and Anna was able to scurry around him. She retrieved Van Helsing's gun from where it had fallen and aimed it at the struggling creature. "We must kill it," she announced.

Van Helsing gripped her wrist, forcing the barrel

of the gun toward the ground. "No. Wait."

The monster crashed to his knees, the powerful sedative in the darts doing its work. "If you value your lives, and the lives of your kind," he moaned, "you *will* kill me." His bleary eyes seemed to plead with them.

"Why?" Van Helsing asked.

"If Dracula finds me . . ." Frankenstein rasped. He was having trouble getting out words now. The sleeping potion in the darts was very potent. He tried again. "I am the key to my father's machine. The key to life. Life for Dracula's children."

"He already awakened them without you," Van Helsing informed the monster. "Last night."

"Those creatures were from just one bride, from one single birth. And they died." His sorrowful eyes gazed straight into Van Helsing's. "Only with me can he give them lasting life."

Van Helsing nodded slowly as Frankenstein's words sunk in. "There are more of those things?"

"Thousands." Then Frankenstein's eyes shut and he passed out, crashing face first into the dirt.

Van Helsing stared at the enormous man, lying on the ground. *It's insane*, he thought. *Impossible. Yet it's true. Dracula intends to power those generators using this poor misshapen, misbegotten creature. And if he*

succeeds . . . Van Helsing shook his head. He didn't want to think the unthinkable.

Anna lifted her gun and aimed at Frankenstein's head. Van Helsing snapped back to attention and stepped in front of her, blocking her shot.

"Get out of the way," she ordered him, anger flashing in her eyes. "You heard what he said. Dracula will use him to complete his foul plan. We have to kill him to prevent that from happening."

Van Helsing struggled to find the words to explain his decision to her. "My life, my job is to vanquish evil. I can *sense* evil." he said. He gestured at Frankenstein. "This thing, this man, whatever it is, isn't evil. Evil may have created it. May even have left its mark on it, but evil does not rule it. So I cannot kill it."

Anna gazed at him steadily, still gripping the gun. "But *I* can."

"Not while I'm here." He had to try to make her understand his position so that they wouldn't become enemies over this. "Your family has spent four hundred years trying to kill Dracula. Maybe this poor creature can help us find a way. If we—"

Van Helsing broke off. Something was not right— his keen senses were telling him evil was near. Van Helsing caught a glimpse of shadow in the shape of a werewolf vanishing into the cavern.

"Oh, no," Anna gasped. "The werewolf, he's seen us." She waved at Frankenstein with the revolver. "Now they know where this creature has been hiding." She looked at Van Helsing, her mouth set in a grim straight line. "They'll come for him, and Dracula will finally have what he wants. Neither you nor I will be able to stop them."

Van Helsing nodded. "I must get him to Rome. We can protect him there."

Anna sighed and handed Van Helsing his gun. "I may regret this, but all right. I won't kill him. We'll do this your way."

TEN

Van Helsing walked with Carl to an ornate coach drawn up in front of Manor Valerious. The huge black horses snorted and stamped, eager to get on the road. Their movements made the kerosene lanterns hanging from the corners of the carriage jangle. Van Helsing was pleased to see how lively the team was. He knew that for his plan to work, they would need all the speed they could muster. These horses seemed fearless and ready to take on any challenge.

Anna stepped out of the coach and hopped down from the running board. "All set," she told Van Helsing.

"Now whatever you do, don't stare at him," Van Helsing instructed Carl.

"What do you take me for?" Carl scoffed. "I have manners. I've seen some things."

Van Helsing smiled at the friar's bravado, knowing

that nothing in Carl's secluded and sheltered life in the monastery would have prepared him for what he was about to see. "Okay," Van Helsing said.

Van Helsing opened the coach door and helped Carl up onto the running board. Carl took one look inside the coach and teetered.

"Carl?" Van Helsing said, watching the little friar's mouth drop open and his eyes practically bug out of his head. Frankenstein's monster sat in the coach on one of the velvet benches, chained to the back wall of the compartment.

"Am I staring?" Carl asked. "Oh, right I'm staring." He leaned to whisper in Van Helsing's ear, "Is that a *man*?"

Van Helsing shoved Carl into the seat opposite Frankenstein. "Actually, it's seven men. Parts of them, anyway. All stitched together."

"Uh . . . interesting."

Frankenstein rattled the chains that bound him. "By exposing me, you have condemned me," he moaned. "Me and all of humanity."

"Keep an eye on him," Van Helsing said. "And if you need to, use this." He handed Carl the blowgun. The friar popped it into his mouth and nodded. Van Helsing had a feeling that the blowgun was now permanently installed in Carl's mouth. The cleric

wasn't going to take any chances.

The monster stomped his feet and cried out, "Free me! Let me fight! Let me die! But do not let me be taken alive."

Carl raised an eyebrow at Van Helsing. Van Helsing shrugged, then stepped out of the compartment. *A more unlikely pair may never be seen again*, Van Helsing decided. If the situation weren't so dire, he'd find putting Carl in charge of Frankenstein humorous. But the fate of humankind could depend on their successfully keeping Frankenstein out of Dracula's clutches.

A few minutes later, Van Helsing took up the reins of a team of carriage horses. "Yah!" he shouted at the team. They charged forward, straining at their leads.

I like their spirit, Van Helsing thought. He enjoyed being at the helm of such a powerful team of horses. The impressive black steeds seemed to sense his urgency and thundered along the road through the woods. He could feel them pushing themselves to greater and greater speeds.

The hairs on the back of Van Helsing's neck tingled as he sensed an evil presence nearby. *I'm being watched*, he realized. He stuck the reins in his mouth and gripped his crossbow, ready to fire. He braced himself for an attack.

He didn't have to wait long. Dracula's bride Verona swooped down and, using her razor-sharp talons, jerked him off his seat, sending the crossbow flying out of his hands. Just as sharply, Van Helsing yanked himself out of her clutches. He slammed down hard on to the lead horse's back. The horse never broke pace but kept charging along the mountain road.

Gripping the horse's flanks with his knees, Van Helsing stayed low, his face beside the horse's neck. He tangled his fingers into the horse's mane and urged the horse on faster. He knew this was merely Verona's way of saying hello. There would be continued attacks for the rest of the journey.

The path he was on led around the mountain. To one side was the dense forest creeping upward. To the other side was the sheer drop of the cliff. The horses were fast approaching a narrow hairpin turn. Dracula's brides, Verona and Aleera, followed above him, soaring in the inky cloud-filled sky.

"Yah!" Van Helsing shouted. "Faster," he cried to the team of sweating, laboring animals. "Faster!"

Van Helsing shot a look back at the coach rattling behind him, then up again at the steep curve ahead.

Van Helsing readied himself, hunkering down even lower on his horse. He took the sharp turn at full

tilt, never letting up on his mount, The entire team clattered around the curve at full speed, their hooves fighting to avoid slipping over the edge. They thundered along the path, kicking up stones and dirt clumps.

Van Helsing clutched his horse determinedly. The angle of the curve was too much for the weight of the coach. He could feel it dragging the team hard to the side as it skittered toward the edge of the cliff. He glanced over his shoulder and saw the carriage careening wildly. Then, just as he had anticipated, the couplings attaching the coach to the team of horses snapped. With a great screech of metal against metal, the coach jerked free—and tumbled over the side of the cliff.

The horses picked up speed as they were released from the weight of the coach, steadying themselves as they ran. Van Helsing pulled himself high on the horse's back to see the coach spiraling through the air, heading for the valley floor far below.

Above him, Aleera and Verona shrieked in horror. "We must not let the creature be destroyed!" Verona screamed.

Van Helsing watched the two brides swoop down toward the plummeting coach. They flew to either side of it, and grabbed it by its frame, but the weight

was too great for them to stop its rapid descent.

"Save him!" Aleera ordered. "Save the monster!"

Aleera lost her grip and tumbled backward in the air, her red hair flying about wildly. Verona clung to the side of the coach, and the coach and the dark-haired vampire bride dropped below Van Helsing's sightline.

"Even *you* can't fight gravity, ladies," Van Helsing said. He grinned on the back of his horse, knowing that his ruse had worked. "I know something you don't know," he taunted under his breath.

The vampire brides were chasing an empty coach.

Well, not quite empty, Van Helsing thought with satisfaction.

Ka-boom! Splintered wood and wheel spokes shot upward as the coach exploded, and then rained down into the valley far below, taking the brides along for the ride.

"Gotta hand it to Carl," Van Helsing said as he slowed the lead horse to a more manageable trot. "Attaching silver stakes to that new and highly explosive glycerin really was a work of genius."

Van Helsing allowed his horses only a few moments to recover, then he urged them to full speed again. He quickly arrived at the prearranged meeting

place and pulled the team of horses to a stop. He had been there less than a minute when a second coach barreled out of the forest. This time it was Anna holding the reins in the driver's seat.

Carl's blond head popped out of the coach window. "Come on!" he cried to Van Helsing. "Hurry!"

Anna barely slowed the team of horses as Van Helsing clambered aboard. He leapt up beside Anna on the buckboard. "I told you the decoy plan would work," he said.

"I wouldn't get too cocky if I were you," she warned.

A throaty growl above them made Van Helsing glance up. "The werewolf!" he shouted above the stampeding horses' hooves. Eight hundred pounds of enraged beast leaped onto the top of the coach, heading straight for Van Helsing and Anna.

A sudden turn in the road threw the werewolf off balance. It skittered sideways across the carriage roof, shattering the lanterns and dousing the coach in kerosene. The werewolf regained its balance and lunged toward Anna and Van Helsing again.

"Watch out!" Van Helsing shouted as he rolled off the driver's seat to the side of the carriage. Anna quickly flung herself the other way.

The werewolf landed on the buckboard, let out a

frustrated yowl, and sprang back up onto the coach roof. It climbed down the back side, just as the flames from the lanterns hit the kerosene.

The roof burst into flame!

"What's going on?" Carl screamed out the window. He spotted Anna clinging to the side of the coach in front of the window.

"Carl!" she shouted. "Help me!"

"Oh, no!" Carl reached through the window and grabbed her arm trying desperately to keep her from dropping off the running board.

"Carl!" Van Helsing cried.

Carl leaned farther out the window and saw that Van Helsing was being dragged behind the coach, his fingers gripping the axle.

"What do I do?" Carl exclaimed. He couldn't let go of Anna and he couldn't get to Van Helsing. His stomach hurt, sweat dripped into his eyes, and his heart pounded frantically.

"I can help," Frankenstein offered.

Carl's head whipped around and he stared at the monster. "You won't kill me?" Carl asked.

"Only if you don't hurry."

"I think I can manage a minute or so," Anna told Carl. "Do what you need to do!"

Carl nodded and fumbled for the keys to

Frankenstein's chains. Nervousness made him clumsy.

Van Helsing grimaced in pain, his five fingers clinging to the axle of the coach. Then four. Then three. Then two. He couldn't hold on anymore. Just as his last finger peeled away from the metal, a huge fist grabbed him by the collar and pulled him out of the path of the rushing wheels.

Van Helsing stared up into Frankenstein's face. Without a word, Frankenstein heaved Van Helsing up onto the buckboard. At the same time, Carl helped Anna swing up next to him.

Flames engulfed the top portion of the carriage, but that didn't deter the werewolf. He was back. Van Helsing glanced over his shoulder and saw the creature looming up above the flames.

A huge fist splintered the forest side of the coach. Frankenstein's head and shoulders burst out of the hole. He bellowed in terror.

Carl's head popped out beside Frankenstein's. "He doesn't like the fire!" he called up to Van Helsing.

"Neither do I!" Van Helsing replied. "So let's get out of here!"

With Frankenstein's help, Carl wriggled out of the smashed side of the coach and onto the running board with Frankenstein close behind him.

"Jump!" Van Helsing cried. Anna leapt from the

driver's seat, rolled several feet, then raced into the dense forest. Carl and Frankenstein followed quickly on her heels.

Van Helsing paused long enough to shoot the bolts out of the axle so that the horses could break free of the flaming carriage. The werewolf let out a furious roar. Van Helsing spun around as he jumped from the carriage, shooting the werewolf in the chest just as it tackled him. They grappled as they landed and rolled in the dirt.

The burning coach careened off the road and crashed into a tree, shattering into pieces. Still Van Helsing fought the rabid werewolf, but finally, the silver bullets did the trick. The werewolf stopped struggling and lay motionless. Van Helsing crawled away and leaned against a nearby tree, panting to catch his breath.

Anna tromped through the forest. She was exhausted, bruised, and dazed from the coach ride. But she had to find Van Helsing and the others. She was pretty certain she had circled back to where she had leapt from the coach.

As she rounded a tree, her breath caught. There, just a few feet ahead of her, lay her brother Velkan. Human again.

She rushed forward and knelt beside him, cringing at the sight of his battered body, and the blood from the terrible wound in his chest. It was obvious that Van Helsing had shot the creature with his special bullets. She stroked her brother's forehead. "Oh, Velkan," she murmured.

Velkan's eyes flicked open. "Anna," he gasped. He gave her a sorrowful look. "Forgive me." His eyes shut again, and she knew that was the last time she would hear his voice.

Anna flung herself onto his battered body. "Velkan," she sobbed. "Oh, Velkan."

Gradually she calmed herself. She took a deep breath and kissed him on the cheek. "I will see you again," she promised.

A movement nearby tore her attention away from her dead brother. Van Helsing staggered toward her.

Fury replaced her sorrow, and Anna charged at Van Helsing. "You killed him!" she wailed, pummeling him with her fists. "You killed him!"

Van Helsing grabbed her wrists, holding her tight. "Now you know why they call me a murderer," he said sadly.

Anna looked into his eyes and saw the sadness in them. She nodded slowly, and Van Helsing released her. She knew he had not done this deed lightly, and

that it was the only possible choice he could have made.

Van Helsing crossed away from her to gaze down upon Velkan's body. "I'm sorry," he said.

Anna felt a light tap on her shoulder. She turned—and faced a grinning vampire bride. Aleera had managed to escape the coach's explosion. Verona had not been so lucky.

"Aleera!" she cried. Anna had barely gotten out the vampire bride's name when she was lifted off the ground. Aleera had moved so quickly Van Helsing was caught off guard. He dashed toward her, but Anna was too high in the air for him to reach.

"Help!" Anna cried. Aleera soared away, taunting Van Helsing the entire time, her long red hair streaming out behind her.

Van Helsing raced after them, furious that he'd let his guard down for even a moment. He broke through the trees and found himself at the edge of a cliff. Frankenstein and Carl slowly came up beside him, still recovering from their close call with the werewolf.

Van Helsing pointed at the sky. Together, they watched Aleera fly away with Anna toward the lights of a distant city.

ELEVEN

T he three men staggered down an alley, battered and bruised. Van Helsing kept his cloak wrapped around him tightly, favoring one side. Frankenstein's face was hidden within a hood, but Van Helsing knew it was only a matter of time before the creature's enormous size would attract attention. So far they had managed to keep to deserted side streets and shadows, but that wasn't bringing them any closer to finding Anna. Van Helsing was sure they'd need to venture more deeply into the city to find her.

A sudden blast of wind put them all on alert. Van Helsing winced in pain as he reached to grip his gun. Dracula's remaining bride, Aleera, appeared suddenly, and perched on a snowy eave above them. Her red hair was piled on top of her head and held with a jeweled comb. She wore an elegant dress, covered in lace, and a hooded velvet cloak.

"You have been so much trouble to my master,"

she complained, her full deep red lips in a pout. "Now you've killed Verona." She grinned. "Not that I mind. Now I am the only one left, and I will have the Master's undivided attention."

"What do you want?" Van Helsing demanded.

"The Master commands a trade," Aleera replied. "The monster for the princess."

Frankenstein glared at the vampire, and took a step toward her, as if he were going to attack. Van Helsing stopped him. "Somewhere public," Van Helsing told Aleera. "With lots of people."

He could feel Frankenstein's sorrowful eyes upon him, and knew that the creature felt betrayed. The monster had begged to be killed rather than become a tool for Dracula and now Van Helsing seemed to be selling him out.

"We will meet at a place where your master will be less inclined to expose his . . . other side," Van Helsing said.

Van Helsing kept his eyes on Aleera, waiting to see if she would agree to his condition.

Aleera gave his proposal some thought. "I know!" she said, a hideous smile crossing her pale face. "Tomorrow is All Hallow's Eve. Here in Budapest there is a wonderful masquerade ball."

She leapt to the rooftop and clapped her hands. "I

love masquerade balls, don't you?" She narrowed her dark eyes and pointed at Van Helsing. "Vilkova Palace, on the bank of the river," she ordered. "Midnight."

She whooped with giddy, deranged delight and leapt into the air, vanishing over the side of the roof. Her movement created a blast of wind, scattering autumn leaves down on top of Van Helsing, Carl, and Frankenstein.

Van Helsing took in a deep breath, and as he did, searing pain caused him to wince.

"Are you all right?" Carl asked. "Are you hurt?" He reached for Van Helsing's cloak.

Van Helsing shoved the friar's hand away. Frankenstein's eyes narrowed suspiciously. The huge creature lunged forward and yanked the cloak aside, nearly knocking over Van Helsing.

"He's been bitten," Frankenstein boomed. "Bitten by a werewolf."

Carl took a step backward, his eyes growing large as he stared at Van Helsing. Van Helsing pulled his cloak closed again, not saying a word.

"Now you will become one of the creatures you have hunted so passionately," Frankenstein said. "I wonder, will others be so passionate as they hunt you?"

At twilight the following evening, Carl and Van Helsing stepped out of an old, moss-covered mausoleum in the royal graveyard of the Vilkova Palace. Together they shoved the huge stone door shut and lowered the bar into place. Van Helsing double-checked it to be sure it was locked.

"According to the books, you won't turn into a werewolf until the rising of your first full moon, two nights from now. Even then, you'll still be able to fight Dracula's hold over you until the final stroke of midnight."

"Great. Sounds like I have nothing to worry about."

Carl looked at him as if he were a madman, then he got it. "Oh, well, um, that still gives us forty-eight hours to find a solution."

"Right," Van Helsing said.

Carl pulled his mask down over his face and handed Van Helsing his. "Right now we have a party to go to."

Carl adjusted his court jester hat, and Van Helsing donned his silver mask. Then they left the graveyard and headed for the palace. Carl glanced back at the mausoleum. "Are you sure Frankenstein won't be able to get out of there?" he asked.

"Not unless he has help from the dead," Van Helsing replied.

Carl nodded, then murmured a low "wow." The Vilkova Palace was straight ahead, glittering in the last rays of the setting sun. As the moon rose, it shone down on the river behind the castle, and the spires and enormous stained glass windows sparkled. Festive paper lanterns lined the pathway through the formal gardens leading to the palace.

Van Helsing pushed open the heavy doors, and he and Carl entered the palace. Carl gasped at the incredible luxury of the surroundings and the amazing sights everywhere he turned. The grand ballroom was packed with dancing couples and extraordinary decorations. Jugglers, fire eaters, and tightrope walkers performed throughout the ballroom, while an orchestra played strange, hypnotic dance music. All the guests were wearing exotic and elaborate painted masks, and many were dripping with jewels.

An acrobat somersaulted past Carl, nearly knocking the friar over. On his other side, a performer held up a torch and blew the small flame into a roaring fire that almost singed Carl's ear. He jumped and stumbled backward.

"Well, this is different," Carl commented, regaining his balance.

"Dracula must have something up his sleeve," Van Helsing murmured, scanning the crowded party.

"So, in situations like this, do we have a solid plan?" Carl asked. "Or do we just improvise?"

"A bit of both, actually."

They strolled through the dancing couples and arrived at one of the many banquet tables piled high with delectable treats. Van Helsing inhaled deeply.

"Smells wonderful, doesn't it?" Carl said, loading up a gold plate with ham, sausages, and cheeses. He eyed the dessert table laden with pastries, his mouth watering.

"Not everything," Van Helsing replied.

"What do you smell?" Carl asked.

"Everything," Van Helsing said. "Roast boar, spun sugar, juniper bushes, ladies' perfume." He took another whiff. "Oh, yes, and rotted human flesh."

Carl shot him a disgusted look and put his plate down. "You sure do know how to put a damper on the evening."

"Come on," Van Helsing said, heading for the sweeping marble staircase. "Let's get a better view."

Elsewhere in the ballroom, Dracula was dancing with Anna. They were both wearing masks, and Anna had been forced to change from her practical leggings and doublet into an elegant red gown. A glittering

tiara topped her piled-up dark hair, and she wore a jewel-encrusted mask.

"How does it feel to be a puppet on my string?" Dracula asked, his dark eyes burning into her from behind his mask.

Anna strained against his embrace, but it was no use. She was completely within his power.

"I won't let you trade me, Count," she told him. She was determined that he would not get hold of Frankenstein, even if it meant her own death. Those horrible vampire offspring could not be allowed to come to life.

"I have no intention of trading you," Dracula informed her. "And if I know Van Helsing, and I think I do, he isn't planning on making a trade either."

Dracula spun Anna to a mirrored wall. She shuddered when she realized he cast no reflection—she looked as if she were dancing by herself.

"Don't we make a beautiful couple?" he crooned. "I'm looking for a new bride. Someone strong and beautiful. Someone like you. All it takes is one bite from me."

"Never!" Anna exclaimed with disgust. "You make my skin crawl."

Up in the balcony, Carl and Van Helsing peered down at the dance floor. The many dancers, guests,

and performers swirled below them in dizzying patterns. Carl nudged Van Helsing. "There she is," he said, pointing to where Anna was dancing with Dracula.

Van Helsing scanned the glittering ballroom, taking in its layout, the exits, and the routes to Anna. A slow smile spread across his face.

Carl raised an eyebrow. "You have a plan, don't you?" he asked. "I can tell."

"Go down there and distract Dracula," Van Helsing instructed. "Just long enough for me to grab Anna."

"Great," Carl muttered. "I get the vampire and you get the girl."

Van Helsing ignored Carl's comment. "Hightail it away from Dracula and meet us back up here," he added, keeping his eyes glued to Anna. For his plan to work, he'd need to time his moves perfectly.

"Go," he urged Carl, shooing the cleric away.

Carl threw up his hands. "I'm going, I'm going!" He hurried down the marble staircase and wove his way among the costumed crowd to find Dracula.

Down on the dance floor, Carl leapt out of the way of a fire eater, startled by the performer's sudden flaring flame.

It gave him an idea.

As the fire eater demonstrated his skill at swallow-

ing fire and then blowing it into huge flames, Carl hovered nearby, never letting the performer get too far out reach. When the fire eater was in position, Carl shoved him straight at Dracula. The performer stumbled; his flames crackled up the back of Dracula's cape.

Van Helsing watched with satisfaction as Dracula whirled around and flung the unfortunate fire breather across the room. This was Van Helsing's chance.

He jumped up onto the balcony ledge and gripped the tightrope. His movements knocked off the high-wire acrobats, who dropped down onto the floor, creating chaos among the dancers. Van Helsing slashed the tightrope and used it to swoop down to Anna. He grabbed her as the rope swung past her, and together they swung up to the opposite balcony.

The music stopped, and the entire crowd below them looked up at the balcony. Some pointed, others murmured and whispered together. Then, as if on a cue, they all removed their masks.

Van Helsing watched in shock as the faces down below went pale, pale white, their eyes yellowed, and fangs dropped down over their bloodred lips.

"They're vampires!" Anna gasped.

Dracula strode to the center of the ballroom. "Welcome to my summer palace," he called up to Van

Helsing. "So glad you could join me—and several hundred of my closest friends."

A side door from the gardens burst open, and a group of vampires carrying Frankenstein charged into the ballroom. Igor was balanced on the monster's chest.

"We have him, Master!" Igor cried triumphantly. "We have him!"

Dracula laughed an evil laugh of satisfaction. He waved up toward Anna and Van Helsing. "Enjoy yourselves," he told the crowd.

The vampires went wild, shrieking with delight, rushing up to the balcony. The beating of their powerful wings nearly knocked Van Helsing and Anna off their feet. A suit of armor nearby clattered to the floor.

Anna ripped off the arm of the armor and shoved her hand down its metal sleeve and into its metal glove. Attached to the glove was an iron mace, covered with spikes. She raised it to show Van Helsing.

"Let's go!" Van Helsing grabbed her arm and together they raced down a hallway.

"Where are we going?" Anna cried.

"Out! Somewhere!"

"Where's Carl?" she asked, never breaking pace.

"He'll find us. I'm sure of it."

They charged up the stairs and through a set of

double doors, vampires hot on their trail. They each grabbed one of the massive doors, slammed it shut, then bolted it. They could hear the vampires flinging themselves at the door, and quickly it began to splinter.

"Those doors won't slow them down for long," Van Helsing said. Just then, Carl scurried around the corner, holding the lava contraption he had shown Van Helsing back in the armory in Vatican City.

"Now I know what it's for!" he declared. He pulled the pin of the device and placed it on the floor. He glanced around the room. "If they're coming in through that door, and there are more of them down the stairs, how are we getting out of here?" he asked.

"Through that window!" Van Helsing replied. Before Carl could balk, Van Helsing and Anna each grabbed one of his arms and the three of them crashed through a floor-to-ceiling window. Glass splintered and scattered all around them as they dropped down into the watery catacombs below.

Just as they hit the water, a nearly blinding burst of ultraviolet light blasted on in the room they'd just left. The lava contraption was doing its work. The cries of vampires drowned out everything else for the moment, as the evil creatures melted, exposed to the massively powerful artificial sunlight of the weapon.

"Carl, you're a genius!" Van Helsing cried when he popped back up above the surface of the water. He pulled himself up onto the stone walkway.

Carl sputtered and shook his head, spraying water everywhere. "A genius with access to unstable chemicals."

"Look!" Anna cried.

Van Helsing's head whipped around. Igor was shouting orders at a dozen of the fat little Dwergi as they maneuvered a longboat down a ramp up ahead. Frankenstein was chained to the mast of the boat.

Van Helsing raced toward the boat. Carl and Anna scrambled out of the water and chased after him. Once the boat hit the water, the Dwergi began rowing rhythmically, pulling away quickly. They paddled out of the tunnel and into the river. A huge grated gate started to lower down behind them. Igor scrambled up the mast and patted the bound Frankenstein on the head. He grinned out at Van Helsing. "Say good-bye to your friends," Igor taunted.

The metal gate slammed shut right in front of Van Helsing, cutting him off from the river. He stared through the grates. Frankenstein stared back, his face a mask of helplessness, and hopelessness. He let out an anguished howl.

"I'll find you!" Van Helsing called to the monster.

"I'll get you back and set you free! I promise you!"

Anna and Carl arrived beside Van Helsing. Anna gripped Van Helsing's arm. "Come on," she said. "We have to beat them back to Castle Frankenstein."

TWELVE

"They're not here!" Van Helsing stared in astonishment at the empty laboratory in Castle Frankenstein. "It's all gone. The equipment, the files, everything."

Carl and Anna stood stunned in the doorway.

"They must have taken it all to Dracula's lair," Van Helsing said.

"Then we've lost," Anna stated flatly.

"Dracula cannot bring his children to life until the sun sets," Carl pointed out. "We still have time to stop them."

Anna stared at him incredulously. "The sun sets in two hours," she said. "The Valerious family has been trying to find his lair for four hundred years! What makes you think we can find it now in two hours?"

Carl gave her a grin. "I wasn't around for those four hundred years, now, was I?"

Van Helsing nodded and smiled. "Let's give Carl

a chance to do what he does best."

Anna raised an eyebrow. "Explode things?"

"Well, maybe later," Van Helsing replied. "No, I was thinking he could do some research."

Carl tapped his forehead. "And I know just where to start."

Van Helsing, Carl and Anna sat in the tower bedroom of the Manor Valerious. They were surrounded by ancient tomes, artifacts, and relics. The rays of the midday sun were faintly breaking through the cloudy sky.

"So here's what I found out," Carl said. "Count Dracula was actually the son of Valerious the Elder." He looked at Anna. "The son of your ancestor."

Anna shrugged. "Everyone knows that. What else?"

"*We* didn't know that!" Carl protested.

"Go on," Van Helsing instructed.

"Well, it all started in 1462, when Dracula was murdered."

"Does it say who murdered him?" Van Helsing asked.

"No, just some very vague reference to the Left Hand of God." Carl referred back to the thick book on his lap. "Anyway, according to this, when Dracula

died he made a deal with the devil."

"And was given a new life," Van Helsing said, jumping in.

"But the only way to sustain that life was by drinking the blood of others," Anna added.

"Are you two going to let me tell the story?" Carl complained.

"Sorry," Anna said.

"Sorry," Van Helsing echoed, hiding his smile.

"Your ancestor went to Rome for forgiveness," Carl continued. "He felt guilty that this was his own flesh and blood doing such terrible things. That's when the bargain was made. Valerious the Elder was to kill Dracula in return for salvation for his entire family. Right down to you." He nodded at Anna.

Anna nodded back. "But he couldn't do it, could he?" she said. "As evil as Dracula was, my ancestor couldn't kill his own son."

"This is where it gets even more interesting," Carl said. He put down the book and picked up a small painting. "See? This shows that he banished Dracula to an icy fortress, sending him through a door from which there was no return."

"And then the devil gave him wings," Anna said, pointing to an image in the painting.

"Precisely."

"So we've got the background. Now, where do we find this door leading into Dracula's lair?" Van Helsing asked.

"I don't know," Carl admitted. "But here's the good news."

"There's good news?" Van Helsing asked.

"When the old man couldn't kill his child, he left clues, so that future generations might do it for him."

"That must be what my father was looking for up here in the tower room," Anna declared. "Looking for clues to the location of the door."

Van Helsing paced around the room. "The door," he muttered. His eyes narrowed. "The door." He snapped his fingers. "Yes! Of course!"

He turned and dashed out of the tower room. Anna and Carl exchanged an astonished look, then charged after him. They caught up to him in the armory where he stood staring at the enormous painting he'd seen the first night he was here. The map of Transylvania.

"You said your father spent hours staring at this painting, trying to find Dracula's lair," he said, never taking his eyes off the map. "I think you were right. Literally." Van Helsing ran his fingers along the frame of the painting but realized there was none. The painting was molded onto the wall.

119

"I think *this* is the door," Van Helsing explained. "He just didn't know how to open it."

Carl pointed at the Latin inscription on the painting. "Maybe that inscription works like the painting in the tower that came to life." He began mumbling as he worked to translate the ancient words.

Anna shook her head. "If this was a door, my father would have opened it long ago."

Carl shoved a chair aside, revealing that a piece of the painting was torn away. "I can't finish the inscription. It's incomplete."

"That's why your father couldn't open the door," Van Helsing said. He reached into his coat pocket and pulled out the canvas that the Cardinal had given him back in Vatican City. "He didn't have this."

"Where did you get that?" Anna asked, her eyes wide.

"Your ancestor left it with the Order years ago." He handed the cloth to Carl. "Finish it."

Carl placed the painted fabric into position on the map. It fit perfectly. *"Deum lacessat ac ianuam imbeat aperiri,"* he intoned in Latin.

"In the name of God, open this door," Van Helsing translated.

The painting began to change. A thick crystal frost spread out from the frame toward the center.

Quickly, the entire canvas was dissolved by the ice, leaving an ancient mirror in its place.

Carl's mouth dropped open. "A mirror?"

Anna stared at the mirror too. "Dracula has no reflection in a mirror," she remembered.

"Why, I wonder," Van Helsing said.

Carl turned to face them. "Maybe . . . maybe to Dracula, it's not a mirror at all!"

Van Helsing reached out to touch the mirror. His hand went straight through it, vanishing up to his wrist! He inhaled sharply.

"What's wrong?" Carl asked.

"It's cold!" Van Helsing pulled back his hand. It was covered in snow. "And it's snowing, I see."

Van Helsing grabbed one of the torches hanging in a sconce on the stone wall. "See you on the other side!" he said.

"Don't worry," Carl assured him nervously. "We're right behind you! Well, maybe not *right* behind you . . ."

"Be careful," Anna told Van Helsing.

"I will be." He stepped through the mirror, vanishing inside it.

THIRTEEN

On the other side of the mirror Van Helsing found himself in a completely different landscape. A snowy, ice-covered world. He stared up at an enormous fortress chiseled out of the frozen mountain.

"Castle Dracula," Anna said as she stepped up beside him.

"Where's Carl?" Van Helsing asked.

"He was right behind me," Anna said.

They turned and looked at the mirror that led back into Anna's family castle. A moment later Carl stepped through the frame with his eyes closed. They popped open when he felt the change in temperature, and then widened as he gazed up at the huge castle looming above them.

Without a word, he whirled around and ran right back into the mirror.

Wham! Carl didn't go through the mirror; instead

he slammed into it and fell backward onto the icy ground.

"I guess it's a one-way ticket," he commented.

"Come on," Van Helsing said. "We've got work to do." They carefully made their way across the slippery, jagged landscape.

"Do you have a plan?" Carl asked nervously. "I definitely prefer it when there's a plan."

They stopped in front of the massive entrance to the ancient fortress. The iron door was rusted shut and covered in slick ice.

"We're going to go in there and stop Dracula," Van Helsing said. "That's the plan."

"And kill anything that gets in our way," Anna added.

"Let me know how that goes for you," Carl said. He began backing away. One look from Van Helsing stopped him.

"Kidding," Carl said sheepishly. "Just show me the way in."

Van Helsing scanned the looming icy façade. He pointed to a transom above the enormous double doors. "We might be able to slip through there," he said.

Carl raised his eyebrows. "Sure. If we could fly like Dracula. It's only thirty feet up, after all."

123

Van Helsing flung out his arms and grabbed Carl and Anna by their collars. With a howling shout, he lifted them into the air. Running straight up, he shattered the glass transom and the three of them crashed through.

They landed with a thud inside the castle. Anna and Carl scrambled to their feet and stared incredulously at Van Helsing. He knew they were stunned by his amazing—and brand-new—ability.

"A little trick I've picked up," Van Helsing joked.

"Hm." Carl eyed Van Helsing curiously. "As grateful as I am to be out of the cold, this new skill of yours doesn't seem like a very good thing."

Van Helsing nodded, knowing that his astonishing strength came from the werewolf blood beginning to course through his veins. And once it took over entirely—

"Oh!" He doubled over in pain.

Anna gently touched his arm. "Are you okay?"

Van Helsing nodded. He pulled himself together, and forced himself to stand back up again.

Anna gasped.

Van Helsing's fingers flew to his face. He could feel his features contorting. *The wolf,* he thought.

Almost immediately, his skin and muscles spasmed, and then his face returned to its normal shape.

The experience had only lasted a moment, but it was enough. He could not deny it—the transformation would take place. It was already beginning.

Anna cleared her throat and Van Helsing gave her a sad, wry smile. "Let's get to work."

Van Helsing strode into the vast icy room. He pulled flaming torches from the walls and handed one to Anna, one to Carl, and then took one for himself. He lifted it high to illuminate their surroundings.

They stood in the grand entry foyer of Dracula's castle. Van Helsing figured the room could hold the entire population of Anna's hometown. And everywhere he looked—at the massive pillars, the walls that soared into the upper atmosphere, the enormous chandeliers dripping icicles—every single surface was covered with disgusting, gooey vampire cocoons.

Anna stepped up beside Van Helsing. "Oh, no," she murmured, gazing all around her. "If he brings all of these to life . . ."

"The world will be a big vampire buffet," Carl finished for her.

Just then, Van Helsing sensed a sudden movement in the corner. Igor, Dracula's servant, raced across the frozen floor, a bundle of electrical equipment and wires in his misshapen hands. When he caught sight of Van Helsing, his crooked jaw dropped open. The

deformed man was moving so quickly, he had trouble slowing down on the slick floor. He skidded to a stop a few feet away from Van Helsing.

"How— How did you—?" Igor stammered. "It's impossible!"

Igor dropped everything in his hands, spun around, and raced away, skidding and slipping as he went. In a flash, Van Helsing had one of his saw blades in his palm. He flung it at Igor. The weapon whistled through the frigid air and caught Igor's sleeve, pinning him to the rock wall.

Igor struggled to yank himself free, but the saw blade's teeth were sunk deep into the granite and ice surface. As he watched Van Helsing approach, Igor's knees buckled. "Please don't kill me," he whined. "Please!"

Van Helsing strode forward. "Give me one reason why I shouldn't."

Igor wrung his hands, cowering and whimpering. "Well, I . . . er . . . um."

A loud bellowing cry made everyone jump.

"It's Frankenstein!" Carl said.

"And he's close by," Anna added, dashing to the barred window near Van Helsing. Now they could hear chains rattling and groaning gears, along with Frankenstein's shouts. Van Helsing thrust his torch

through an opening between the bars.

Down below them, the monster was encased in a huge block of ice, with only his head and neck free. Chains ran through the ice and were attached to a pulley system.

"It's some kind of elevator shaft," Van Helsing observed.

"Bring me the monster!" a voice called above them, the cry echoing through the shaft.

"Dracula," Van Helsing hissed.

"My master has awakened!" Igor rubbed his hands together and snickered.

The pulley cranked into gear and the chains went taut. Slowly the ice block began to rise.

Van Helsing flung himself at the bars. He yanked and pulled at them furiously. His new strength allowed him to bend them, but not enough to break through to free Frankenstein from his ice prison.

Frankenstein rose to meet Van Helsing's eyes. "There is a cure," the creature whispered.

"What?"

"Dracula has the cure. To remove the curse of the werewolf."

The ice block pulled away from Van Helsing. Desperate to hear more, Van Helsing shoved his head between the twisted metal bars.

"Go!" Frankenstein yelled. "Find the cure. Save yourself!"

Van Helsing gazed up at the bottom of the block of ice. He dragged his head back through the bars.

"You heard him," Anna said, clutching Van Helsing's arm. "Let's go find that cure!"

Van Helsing turned to face her. "I don't get it," he said. "Why would Dracula have a cure?"

"I don't care," Anna said.

"I care," Van Helsing said. "I think it's important."

He crossed to Igor. Carl now had him pinned to the ground. Van Helsing stood over the sniveling man. "Why does Dracula need a werewolf antidote?"

Igor clamped his mouth shut and shook his head.

Van Helsing's eyes narrowed with fury. But before he tried beating the answer out of Igor, Carl bounced up and down on his booted feet. "I know why!" he cried. "I know!"

Van Helsing and Anna stared at the excited friar. The man was practically leaping out of his own skin.

Carl chortled with glee. "Don't you see? It's because the only thing that can kill Dracula is a *werewolf*!"

Van Helsing's brow furrowed. "Are you sure?"

Carl nodded enthusiastically. "That's what the painting meant in Anna's family castle. The one that

came alive! It was showing the battle between the vampire and the werewolf!"

"But Dracula has been using werewolves to do his bidding for centuries," Anna protested. "If they are his only real enemy, why would he do that?"

"If one ever had the will to turn on him," Carl explained, "Dracula would need a cure to remove the curse. Then he could turn the poor fellow back into a regular human before he could bite Dracula."

Anna and Van Helsing gaped at each other, knowing that he was the werewolf who would turn on Dracula.

Snapping into action, Van Helsing turned to Igor. "You're going to take these two and lead them to the antidote," he ordered, nodding toward Anna and Carl.

"No, I'm not," Igor stated.

Van Helsing brought a knife blade up to Igor's throat.

"Why, yes I am," Igor said.

"I thought you'd see it my way," Van Helsing said, sliding the knife back into its sheath. He faced Anna and Carl. "And I'll go after Dracula."

"Are you insane?" Anna demanded.

Van Helsing shrugged. "Not yet."

"He's right," Carl told Anna. "When the bell begins to toll midnight, he will have the ability to kill

Dracula. We just have to find the cure and get it to Van Helsing before the final stroke chimes."

Now Anna gawked at Carl. "Are *you* insane?"

"Actually, I've always sort of wondered," Carl admitted.

Van Helsing pulled a small device from one of his pockets. He held it up so that Igor could see the nasty-looking thing—a type of clippers clearly meant to inflict pain.

"Every time you hesitate," Van Helsing warned Igor, waving the clippers in front of Igor's twisted face, "if they even for a moment suspect that you are misleading them—"

He handed the clippers to Anna. "Clip off one of his digits," he instructed her.

"My pleasure," Anna replied.

"Just make sure to leave him with enough toes to get you there," Van Helsing added.

In spite of the Arctic temperature in the castle, sweat beaded up on Igor's frightened brow. He gestured frantically to the staircase. "The stairs on the right," he said. "They lead to the Black Tower. That's where the antidote is kept."

"What about the stairs on the left?" Van Helsing asked.

Igor bit his lip. Van Helsing held his hand out

toward Anna for the clippers.

"That leads to the Devil's Tower!" Igor shrieked. "Don't hurt me!"

"And what's in the Devil's Tower?" Van Helsing demanded.

"That's where we reassembled Frankenstein's laboratory," Igor confessed.

Van Helsing studied Igor's twisted face. His eyes narrowed as he tried to determine if the evil servant was telling him the truth.

Igor grimaced under Van Helsing's steady scrutiny. "Would I lie to you?" he whined.

"Not if you want to live," Van Helsing said.

"Oh, I do. I do indeed," Igor said.

"Good." Van Helsing turned to Carl. "There are twelve strokes to midnight."

"Yes," Carl said. "That's how you know it's midnight."

"If I'm not cured by the twelfth stroke," Van Helsing said, reaching into his cloak, "use this." He pulled out a silver stake.

Carl's eyes widened. "I—I don't think I could," he whispered.

Van Helsing clapped the stake into Carl's hand. "You must."

Carl nodded, and slipped the stake into a pocket.

He stepped over to Igor and grabbed his collar. "Come on." He dragged Igor to the staircase.

Van Helsing stepped up to Anna. He could see fear and courage in her eyes, and wondered if he wore the same expression.

"Don't worry," she assured him. "We'll find it, and we'll be there on time."

Anna squeezed his arm.

Van Helsing nodded. He wanted her to know he had faith in her, but he couldn't find the right words. Instead, he leaned down and kissed her. When they parted, she looked deeply into his eyes before turning on her heels and dashing after Carl.

FOURTEEN

Igor led Anna and Carl up the staircase to a landing with an arched doorway. "That leads into the Black Tower," he explained. "That's where the antidote is kept."

"What are we waiting for?" Carl said.

Igor and Carl hovered just outside the archway as Anna stepped into the circular tower room. In the center was a huge pedestal holding a large glass jar. Inside the jar was a syringe, suspended in clear jelly-like goo.

Anna headed for the jar.

"Be careful opening that," Carl cautioned from behind her. He stepped in front of Igor. "You don't know what that goop is inside. Hey!"

Anna whirled around to see why Carl shouted. Igor had kicked the friar, sending him sprawling into the room.

Igor cackled gleefully. "Stay as long as you like!" he

chortled. He pulled a lever and a gate crashed down in front of them.

Anna and Carl were locked inside the tower room.

"Toodle-oo!" Igor called over his twisted shoulder as he hurried away.

"I'm sorry," Carl said as he scrambled off the floor. "I only took my eyes off him for a second."

"Let's worry about that later," Anna said. She approached the jar. Up close, the goo looked seriously disgusting. Kind of a cross between mucous and Jell-O. She turned to Carl. "Go ahead," she said. "Grab it."

"*You* grab it," Carl protested. "If there's one thing I've learned, it's never be the first one to stick your hand into a viscous material."

"Smart boy," a woman's voice crooned above them.

Anna and Carl whirled around and discovered Aleera hanging upside down from the rafters, her long red hair reaching toward the floor. Carl let out a yelp and stumbled backward.

Aleera jumped down in front of Carl. "Awww, did I scare you?" she asked him.

"N—n—n—noo," Carl stammered.

Aleera pouted. "Gee. I guess I'd better try a little harder."

Anna whipped out her sword and knocked over

the jar holding the antidote. It crashed to the ground, shattering into pieces. The goo splattered everywhere, and a bit splashed onto Aleera.

"Nooooo!" Aleera howled in pain. The goo burned into her pale flesh like acid. It even burned through the stone floor.

"I told you that stuff could be dangerous," Carl said.

"Grab it!" Anna cried. She pointed to the syringe rolling across the floor. She kept her sword aimed at Aleera, who lay crumpled on the floor.

"Got it!" Using the hem of his frock, Carl reached down and scooped up the syringe. The syringe singed his robe, eating through the fabric.

"Yikes!" Carl hopped around, trying to avoid being burned, but not wanting to drop the syringe. His fabric-wrapped fingers clutched the antidote. "Okay, I've got it again!"

Keeping her eye on Aleera, Anna grabbed the bottom of the broken jar with the antidote in it and scooped up some of the goo. She flung it at the iron bars on the gates blocking the doorway. A hole melted in the center of the metal bars, barely big enough to crawl through.

Carl raced to the arched doorway and Anna helped shove him through. "Go, go, go!" she shouted.

She knew they had to get out of there before Aleera recovered.

"I'm going, I'm going, I'm going!" Carl stumbled out of the hole and raced down the hallway.

Anna lifted her booted foot to climb out when a powerful hand grabbed her shoulder.

"Where do you think you're going?" Aleera demanded. She spun Anna around.

To Anna's horror, the acid burns on the vampire's beautiful face were already healing.

"Keep running, Carl!" Anna shouted.

"You can't go until I say you can go," the vampire said. "And I won't say so until you're dead!"

"Let me go!" Frankenstein bellowed. He had been released from the ice block, and was now strapped into the iron pod.

Dracula stalked the laboratory, checking dials and pulling levers. The entire room sparked into life. Spectacular arcs of electricity shot up and down the walls as the gears kicked in. Fan belts snapped taut and started spinning. Frankenstein howled louder.

"What are you complaining about?" Dracula taunted. "This is why you were made. To prove that life can be *manufactured*!"

Dracula flipped a switch. Frankenstein's pod rose

toward the skylight. "And now," Dracula continued, "you will give that life to my offspring!"

From his hiding place behind the now empty ice block, Van Helsing could see all of the equipment accelerating wildly. The Dwergi raced around the lab, trying to keep things from spinning out of control. Dracula seemed to be in rapture as sparks rained down upon them all.

Van Helsing glanced up to the skylight. He judged it to be about sixty feet up. That was where the pod imprisoning Frankenstein was heading.

Frankenstein thrashed and moaned on the pod as lightning flashed across the sky above him.

Van Helsing climbed straight up the wall, something he would never have been able to do before today. He reached the scaffolding and came face-to-face with a Dwerger.

Before the ugly creature could give him away, Van Helsing grabbed the Dwerger with one hand and chucked him down into one of the dark corners of the laboratory.

Van Helsing scurried across the platform. The wind whipped into a frenzy as the storm raged. He reached the pod, and gazed at Frankenstein.

"I told you I'd get you out of here," Van Helsing told the creature. He studied the pod. Metal straps

were bolted to Frankenstein's chest, holding him into place. "This is going to hurt," he warned.

"I am accustomed to pain," Frankenstein replied.

Van Helsing nodded. "Sometimes it's the pain that lets you know you're alive."

Van Helsing grabbed one of the metal straps holding down Frankenstein. With his newfound, supernatural strength, he ripped it from Frankenstein's chest.

Before Van Helsing grabbed the next strap, a bolt of lightning struck the conductor above the pod. The electricity shot through the pod and into Frankenstein. Frankenstein roared with pain.

Far below, Dracula watched as the burst of energy rushed from the pod and through the wiring in the lab. The equipment instantly overloaded, sending out sparks and flames. The Dwergi frantically tried to maintain control.

Dracula stood in the center of the room, arms outstretched. "Give me life!" he cried.

Van Helsing began to work faster. He had to make sure Dracula's cocoons didn't come to life. He ripped another metal strap from Frankenstein.

"Look out," Frankenstein warned. Van Helsing threw himself to the floor of the scaffolding as another lightning bolt struck the conductor. Frankenstein howled again with pain.

Lying flat on the platform, Van Helsing peered down to see Dracula gloating in the lab below them.

"One more lightning bolt like that and my children shall live!" Dracula shouted to the heavens. Then his eyes locked onto Van Helsing's.

Van Helsing watched as Dracula's expression went from shock to fury. In a moment, Dracula transformed into a hideous winged beast.

Van Helsing quickly ripped off the last metal strap holding down Frankenstein.

"*Ooof!*" Something knocked Van Helsing off his feet. He tumbled over the edge of the platform and dropped down sixty feet into the lab.

Van Helsing peered back up to the skylight. Dracula was transforming from his vile vampire form back into his human shape. He strode toward the pod.

Frankenstein sat up in the pod. To Van Helsing, the creature seemed dazed. Frankenstein was moving slowly, looking around.

"Get out of the pod!" Van Helsing shouted up to the creature. His voice barely carried above the storm.

Another crackling lightning bolt struck the conductor. Electricity coursed through Frankenstein, catapulting him through the air.

"That's three!" Dracula cheered. "My children are coming alive!"

Carl stared at the thick stone bridge connecting the Black Tower he was in to the Devil's Tower he needed to get to. He gazed at the calamitous sky. Thunder crashed, lightning shattered the darkness, and rain pelted him with the force of hailstones. It was not encouraging. Yet the worst sound of all was the horrible chittering of Dracula's offspring. They had come alive!

He stepped out onto the bridge and forced himself not to look down. One false move and he'd tumble over the side of that sheer drop. He would take this slowly.

"Haste makes waste," he murmured. He carefully placed one foot in front of the other as he made his way across the slippery stones.

"*Yahhh!*" Igor shrieked behind him.

Driven on by the cattle prod Igor poked him with, Carl picked up his robes so that he wouldn't trip over them, and raced toward the castle. He could hear Igor's footsteps thudding behind him.

"Huh?" A startling sight stopped Carl in his tracks. Frankenstein was swinging wildly on a cable dangling from the side of the castle.

And he was heading straight toward Carl!

Carl flung himself to the ground, just as

Frankenstein swooped overhead. The huge creature slammed right into Igor and knocked the hunchback over the side of the bridge. Carl winced as he listened to Igor scream the whole way down. Then . . . silence. He carefully pushed himself back up to his feet.

He heard Frankenstein bellow again. Carl peered in the direction of the sound. He spotted the creature still clutching the cable, which had caught in a rock crevice. Frankenstein now hung out over the deep chasm, the cable trapped at an awkward angle.

As Carl watched, Frankenstein slipped down a few feet. Carl could see he was losing his grip.

"Hold on!" Carl cried. "If we can get you some momentum, you can swing back over here!"

Carl hurried to the side of the Black Tower and grabbed the thick cable. With a loud grunt, he yanked it hard, while Frankenstein kicked and squirmed. Finally, the cable broke free. The sharp jerking motion set the cable swinging again. Carl gave it another strong yank. Frankenstein made a swooping arc—and crashed in through one of the windows of the Black Tower where Anna and Aleera were fighting.

Carl stared at the shattered window in amazement. "I couldn't have aimed better if I had tried," he commented. "Well, at least he's all right, for now."

His expression darkened as he thought of Anna,

trapped in the tower with Aleera. Then he shook off his fear and gripped the syringe. He had to get to Van Helsing immediately!

At that same time, up in the Black Tower, Aleera circled Anna.

"Stay away from me," Anna cried. She grabbed a torch and shoved it into Aleera's face.

Aleera giggled, then blew out the flame. Laughing, she blew out every single candle and torch in the room until Anna stood in pitch blackness.

She began groping her way to the archway. She needed to stay out of Aleera's clutches.

"Do you know, being a vampire has so many advantages," Aleera purred. "One of them is the ability to see in the dark."

She's right in front of me, Anna realized. *How does she move so quickly?*

"Of course," the vampire continued, "you mustn't forget our useful power of transformation."

A crash of lightning illuminated Aleera for just a moment. In that brief second Anna could see that Aleera had turned into her grotesque winged form.

Anna leapt to one side, but Aleera was too quick for her. The vampire gripped Anna's neck with her powerful talons.

"I'm going to enjoy this," Aleera whispered. This close, Anna could smell the vampire's foul breath. She fought back her terror as she watched Aleera's sharp teeth descend.

Crash! The tower window shattered as if it had exploded!

Aleera shrieked and released Anna. Anna stumbled backward and tumbled to the floor. She flung her long dark hair out of her eyes, trying to figure out what had happened.

"Frankenstein!" she cried.

The huge creature had crashed through the tower room window!

Frankenstein slipped off the cable he rode in on, and grabbed Aleera by her red hair. Anna leapt to her feet and dashed over to help in the fight.

"No," Frankenstein ordered. "Go and help Van Helsing." He flung Aleera across the room as if she were a rag doll. "Now!" he shouted at Anna, as she stood there motionless.

She knew he was right. Van Helsing would need help battling Dracula.

"Thank you," Anna told Frankenstein. She leapt up to the window.

Anna heard a scuffle and then Frankenstein howled behind her. Anna wasn't sure if it was in anger

or in pain but she forced herself not to look back. *Stay focused*, she told herself. She saw that the castle wall was rough, with plenty of hand- and footholds. She would climb down to the bridge and get over to the other tower. Ignoring the battle in the room behind her between Frankenstein and Aleera, she lowered herself out the window.

"Anna!" Carl cried from his spot on the bridge. "Down here!"

Anna clung to the wall, the rain soaking her to the skin. Shoving her fingers deep into a crevice, she glanced down to Carl. "Why haven't you gotten the antidote to Van Helsing?" she demanded.

"I can't get inside," Carl shouted up to her. "I'll throw it to you, and you swing over to one of the windows."

Anna climbed to a narrow ledge so that she could turn around. She scanned the area. The cable Frankenstein had used to crash in through the window was within reach. If she pushed off very hard, she might be able to get enough of a swing to get to the other side of the bridge.

"Should work," she decided. "If we're very, very lucky." She froze for an instant as the clock chimed once.

"I have complete faith in you!" Carl told her. "And

don't worry—I have excellent aim." The clock chimed again.

Anna grabbed the cable. She took a deep breath and then pushed herself away from the wall. She swung out over the bridge toward the Devil's Tower.

"Three!" Carl shouted as he tossed her the syringe and the clock chimed

She caught the syringe neatly and swung back to her starting place. Anna gripped the cable again. "Now I need to make it all the way across." She bent her knees and pushed off even harder. The fourth chime rang out.

Carl's smile froze. "Look out!" he cried up to Anna.

Aleera swooped out of the castle and snapped Anna's cable!

Anna crashed down onto a jutting rock ledge just below the bridge. The clock tower chimed again.

Aleera landed on the ledge beside Anna. Anna realized there was nowhere to go but down into the chasm. And judging by the gleam in Aleera's red-rimmed eyes, the vampire knew it too.

"Ahh, Anna," the vampire crooned. "After I kill you, your blood will make me even more beautiful. What do you think of that?"

An object whistled past Anna's face, its breeze stirring her dark hair.

Thwump! A silver stake impaled Aleera in the chest.

The vampire's eyes widened in horror. She let out an agonizing wail.

Anna's head whipped around. Carl gave her a little wave. He had climbed down into one of the bridge supports.

"You want to know what I think?" Anna asked the dying vampire. "I think if you're going to kill somebody, kill them. Don't stand around all day talking about it."

Aleera's flesh melted away, and finally, she burst into rot, sending the silver stake flying. It impaled itself into a beam of the bridge just by Carl's head.

"Good work, Carl," Anna said.

"I told you I had excellent aim," he replied. He yanked the stake from the beam and slipped it into a pocket.

The clock in the tower chimed again. "How many is that?" Carl asked, his voice rising in panic. "I've lost count."

"Eight," Anna told him grimly.

FIFTEEN

In the laboratory in the Black Tower, Dracula leapt down from the platform holding the pod. He landed directly in front of Van Helsing. "You're too late, my friend. Your plot has failed. My children live!"

Van Helsing gazed steadily at the vampire. "Then the only way to kill them is to kill you."

A smug expression crossed Dracula's face. "That is correct."

Van Helsing glanced out the window to the clock tower. The enormous hands were at midnight. "So be it," Van Helsing growled.

At the first clock chime, Van Helsing's entire body convulsed. "One," he moaned, his voice more animal than human. Agonizing pain shot through him as his muscles expanded and contracted, creating the shape of the wolf. His flesh felt electrified as his human form began to melt away. The transformation was underway.

Dracula stepped backward, stunned. "No. This . . . this is not right! This cannot be!"

Van Helsing moved toward Dracula. Now his fingers fused into paws. Claws sprouted from the tips.

Dracula composed himself. "You and I are part of the same grand game," he said.

Dracula's voice was calm, but Van Helsing could smell the fear underneath. This heightened sense was another side effect of the werewolf blood.

"We need not find ourselves on opposite sides," Dracula continued, clearly playing for time. Time that Van Helsing wasn't going to give him. He lunged at Dracula.

Dracula instantly transformed into an enormous bat and flew toward the open skylight. The werewolf bounded up after him, ripping its way straight up the sheer rock. With a howl, the werewolf leapt at the vampire. It knocked the winged creature into the lab equipment, setting off more sparks.

Dracula broke free, and became the count again. "You're being used!" he shouted at the werewolf. "As was I! But I escaped and so can you!"

Van Helsing ignored the vampire's words and sprang at Dracula. Dracula transformed back into his winged form. Using its razor-sharp talons, the vampire clawed the werewolf. Van Helsing howled in pain,

then lashed out at the winged beast. The vampire bat shrieked, then flew up into the rafters. It perched above Van Helsing and transformed into Dracula once more. He crouched in the rafters, nursing a limp and bloodied arm.

"I know who you are," Dracula said. "Who controls you. Join me. Join me, and I will cut the strings that tie you to your keepers. I'll give you your life back."

The werewolf crawled straight up the wall, then crept along the rafters toward the vampire.

Dracula was breathing heavily now. The battle had taken its toll. "Don't you understand?" he panted. "Four hundred years ago we were friends! Partners!"

The clock chimed again. The werewolf leapt at Dracula. Dracula transformed again, and tried to fly away. But he was too weak, and fluttered to the ground. Van Helsing dropped down beside him and grabbed the vampire by the throat.

Just then, the werewolf paws transformed back into human hands. He was Van Helsing again. He staggered backward a few feet.

"Wh—" Van Helsing felt dazed. *What happened?* he wondered. *They didn't give me the antidote yet.* His eyes flicked to the window behind Dracula. The thick clouds had completely covered the full moon.

"By the way," Dracula said, his eyes glinting evilly, "did I mention that it was you who killed me, all those years ago?"

"That's impossible!' Van Helsing said. "You were killed over four hundred years ago."

Van Helsing backed away from Dracula, his head spinning. He didn't want to hear anything this creature said to him. It was too confusing. Everything seemed to conspire to make him insane! The werewolf blood, the flames flicking at the short-circuited equipment, the lightning crashes. And worst of all—the awful sounds of the multitudes of the vampire offspring.

"All I wanted was life," Dracula crooned, cutting through the din. "And now I'll have to take yours. And I'd like my ring back, as well." He held up his hand, and Van Helsing saw that it was missing its ring finger. Then Dracula nodded at the ring that Van Helsing wore.

Van Helsing stared down at the ring, turning it around on his finger. *How can this be his?* Van Helsing wondered. *Why can't I remember where I got it from?* The clock chimed again.

"Don't be afraid," Dracula said, his voice soothing and silky.

Van Helsing discovered he had backed up against

a wall. He was trapped. Exhaustion made him breathe hard, made him feel weak, worked against him. He didn't move as he watched Dracula's teeth extend into fangs.

"Now I will give you back your life," Dracula said. "What you want most: your memory."

Van Helsing's eyes bored deep into Dracula's searching for some kind of answer. Then he tore his eyes away—he didn't want Dracula's power to confuse him further. He glanced at the window and saw that the clouds had moved away from the moon. He'd be a werewolf again in a moment.

He made his decision. It was more important to rid the world of this evil than it was for him to learn the truth of his own past.

"Sorry, Dracula," Van Helsing said. "Some things are best left forgotten."

Van Helsing flung his head back and howled as the full moon reappeared. This time the transformation was quick—quicker than Dracula could anticipate. The werewolf lunged at Dracula and sunk his fangs deep into the vampire's throat.

"Aaggghh!" Dracula screeched in agony. He struggled desperately against the werewolf's powerful grip. But the werewolf was too strong. It never let go as Dracula writhed and convulsed. The howling was

deafening, as the vampire rotted and decayed until it shriveled into nothing but dust.

A horrible sound filled the air as the vampire offspring exploded everywhere.

The werewolf pawed the charred remains of the vampire burning into the floor. The clock chimed again.

Anna burst into the lab. She raced toward the werewolf, holding up the syringe. The clock chimed again.

The werewolf whirled around, its yellow eyes filled with the fury of a predator. It leapt on top of Anna, knocking her to the ground. "Twelve," she said.

"That was midnight!" Carl shouted as he ran into the lab. "Did we make it?"

He skidded to a stop, staring at the sight of the werewolf on top of Anna. "Oh, no!"

With shaking hands, Carl pulled the silver stake out of his robes. As much as he hated it, he knew what he had to do. Van Helsing himself had ordered it. He lifted the stake high in the air and hurried to the werewolf. "God forgive me," he whispered.

The werewolf whirled around and gripped Carl's raised arm. Terrified, Carl gazed into the werewolf's eyes. Then his eyes traveled down to the syringe sticking out of the werewolf's chest. It was empty.

The werewolf released the friar and Carl stumbled backward. He realized that Anna was not moving.

The werewolf stared down at her.

"She's dead," Carl said softly.

The werewolf crouched down beside Anna. The full moon streamed through the window, illuminating the beautiful, heroic woman. Her eyes gazed upward, unseeing. The werewolf tipped back his head and howled a long, mournful howl. Carl could feel the anguish, the sorrow, and the loss in that howl, and it sent shivers through him. It was the saddest sound Carl had ever heard.

Slowly, painfully, the antidote did its work. The werewolf transformed back into Van Helsing, as he cried out in anguish at the moon.

It was all over.

EPILOGUE

Van Helsing and Carl stood on a bluff over-looking a calm and beautiful sea. Before them, Anna lay on a funeral pyre, surrounded by flaming torches. Tears streamed down Carl's face as he said the service.

Van Helsing placed another torch at the head of the pyre. He reached out and stroked Anna's long, dark hair. Swallowing hard, he composed himself by staring out to sea. He spotted a familiar figure down below paddling a makeshift raft.

Frankenstein doffed his hat in respect. Van Helsing nodded, and then the creature paddled away. With the strength of Frankenstein's sympathy, Van Helsing felt he could face Anna again, so he turned around.

He gasped. The smoke from the torches seemed to form Anna's face! She smiled straight at Van Helsing. Then her face started to float up into the dawn sky, wreathed in the soft tendrils of smoke.

Van Helsing stumbled forward as if he could follow her to the heavens. More indistinct figures appeared beside her, greeting her. Her mother. Her father. Her brother Velkan, now freed of the werewolf curse.

A hand on his arm stopped Van Helsing. He glanced down to see Carl smiling through his tears beside him. "She's gone home. And saved her ancestors," Carl said.

Van Helsing couldn't speak, so he just nodded.

Anna smiled at Van Helsing once more, and then, in a glorious burst of golden light, she and her family swooped up into the sky. They blended into the rosy glow of the fading stars.

Slowly, a deep feeling of peace spread through Van Helsing. Anna was home at last, as Carl had said.

The two men strode to their horses and mounted them. Van Helsing flicked his reins and he and Carl rode across the bluff into a golden dawn.